A Candlelight
Regency Special

D0988471

CANDLELIGHT REGENCIES

LADY NELL

Sandra Mireles

A CANDLELIGHT REGENCY SPECIAL

Published by
Dell Publishing Co., Inc.
1 Dag Hammarskjold Plaza
New York, New York 10017

Dell ® TM 681510, Dell Publishing Co., Inc.

ISBN: 0-440-14675-5

Printed in the United States of America
First printing—November 1981

LADY NELL

Prologue

The morning was dreary and cold, and a north wind raged over the rooftops. In a fashionable town house in the city of London a storm of another kind was raging. The Earl of Melford had just given an ultimatum to his younger son. Andrew Merriweather, a good-looking young man, was standing rigidly near the windows, his hands thrust deep into the pockets of the riding breeches he wore so casually. He refused to answer, and the earl continued.

"I am sorry for all this, Andrew, but my decision is final. You have been raking around town for long enough. No son of mine is going to bring scandal around all our heads while I am able to stand! No man will stand for being cuckolded in front of all the ton, and St. Clair is worse than most. He has killed his man. Aye, and more than once!" His brows bristled with the force of his words.

Upon hearing this, Andrew faced his father and

asked, "Do you think I fear him? Never say that I am afraid to meet him!" he cried scornfully.

The earl stared at his interlaced fingers as his hands rested on his desk for a long moment before saying, "Aye, and what of the lady? Would you bring scandal on her head also? No, it will not be allowed. I want you to consider this marriage I am proposing. I know it is a bitter potion for you to swallow with your well-known penchant for the feminine members of ton. However, the girl *is* very young and she will have nearly everything when the duke is gone. The estate is entailed, but the private fortune will go to the girl. The house and lands will go to a cousin, but the fortune is extensive and you will be well provided in a way that I am not in a position to do. You are well aware that my estates are going to your brother Lucien and your portion is small, to say the least." He raised a hand to stem the flow of wrath he could see gathering on his son's angry countenance. "And remember," he continued, "I have arranged for you to join Sir George Fanshawe in India. By the time you come home, the girl will be a woman grown and ready to set up housekeeping and perhaps you will have sown your wild oats and be ready to settle down."

At last the wild surge of anger burst forth. "Do you think me a dashed fortune hunter, sir? I am not in the market for such ill-gotten gains!" Andrew spat scornfully.

The earl leaned back in his chair and said, "It is not entirely for your convenience that I have planned this marriage, Andrew. The duke and I are old friends, and he wants to settle the girl comfortably with the least amount of trouble. His health is bad and he could pop off at any moment." He shook his head sadly.

The father and son stared at each other for a long silent moment. The earl was determined and his son defiant, although each knew how it would end. After a moment Andrew bowed his head and in acquiescence and said, "So be it, my lord. I will do it."

Several days later an ill-matched party gathered in the library of the duke's fashionable town house. Accompanied by his father and brother, Viscount Lucien Drayton, Andrew Merriweather arrived feeling supremely miserable and violently uneasy. For perhaps the first time in his short, ungoverned career, Andrew was being forced to face the unpleasant consequences of his rakish behaviour.

He had thought very little about the young woman who was to become his bride this night, and a sinking feeling appeared in his stomach when his eyes fell on the plain, gauche girl, dressed in the schoolgirlish gown. Tall for her years, she was as different as the night was from day from the beautiful ladies with whom he usually associated. His eyes kept darting toward the door after that first glance at his fiancée, and he wondered how long it would be before he could decently make his escape.

The bride was in like case this evening. She was feeling shy and tongue-tied in the presence of her groom and remained seated with her head bowed, in a chair placed at the side of the room out of the way. The old gentlemen, parents of the unlucky pair, carelessly reminisced while the viscount leaned against the mantel and watched his brother uneasily.

Although Lady Nell had never met Andrew Merriweather or the viscount, she was well acquainted with their respective reputations. It was the sort of thing that the young ladies whispered about at odd moments when the headmistress was not about. Nell's bosom bow, Fanny Armstrong, always returned to school from a visit overflowing with gossip, for her sister had been presented the previous season and their home was full of the town doings.

Nell had never hoped to meet these rakish gentlemen and was considerably awed by them. She had no way of knowing that her uneasiness was echoed wholeheartedly by her unwilling bridegroom and was relieved when the vicar's booming voice was heard in the hall speaking to a servant. With no mother to guide her, Nell was nearly overcome by the thoughts of her wedding night and only wished to have it over.

A short, stoutish man entered one step behind the butler, and he smiled warmly at the two parents and the viscount before saying, "Well, well, my lords, Your Grace! Such a happy occasion."

The Earl of Melford rubbed his hands together and said irritably, "Well, let's get it over with. No need of speechifying, sir." He turned to his son and the bride. "What are you waiting for, Andrew? Take your places, take your places." His black brows bobbed ferociously.

The young couple lost no time in doing his bidding, and soon they were making their vows with the utmost expediency. Andrew spoke his words firmly without the least hesitation, while Lady Elinor had to be prompted several times to speak louder. When the ceremony ended the vicar waited expectantly, and for a blank moment Andrew had no idea what he wanted. Then with a flush Andrew realized that he was expected to kiss his bride. He complied stiffly, brushing his lips across her cheek, never meeting her eyes at all.

When the toasts were finished, the viscount excused himself and Andrew followed his lead, leaving the house immediately. His bride was surprised, uncertain, and above all, considerably affronted. She turned to his father and asked, "Where is your son going, my lord?"

He raised his bush brows and looked at her ferociously before saying, "What's that? Oh, Andrew. Don't worry your head about him, girl. He will be no trouble to you, just as I promised. He is sailing for India tomorrow. No doubt there are some last-minute preparations he must see to, don't you know." He gave her a friendly smile.

Very much taken aback at her groom's apparent indifference to his bride, Lady Nell's eyes flashed brilliantly as she realized just what her position was to be. She said, "I see." Both gentlemen were surprised by her quiet dignity as she turned to her father and murmured, "Excuse me, Papa. I too, have some preparations to make." And she stalked out the door.

Chapter One

"I can assure you, my dear Benny, that I have every intention of going at once to town to open the house for my dear husband." Lady Elinor, Countess of Melford, spoke with obvious acidity. "Why, it would be unthinkable for my dear husband to return from his long voyage to find an empty house, and his wife not in attendance."

From the recesses of the most comfortable chair in the room, Benny, who it could be seen was a nondescript woman of uncertain age, waved her hands agitatedly and said, "But, my dear Lady Nell, how could you even think of doing such a thing? I mean . . . He, er, his lordship has hardly acknowledged your existence . . ." Her voice trailed off ineffectually as she saw the expression on her dear Nell's face.

"Exactly," said Nell, her emerald eyes glowing brilliantly. "I mean to make him know I am to be reckoned with, Benny. He had no right to neglect me for all these years," she cried angrily. And indeed she had cause for complaint. After a short wedding eight years previous, she had heard nothing from her bridegroom other than a message of condolence delivered when her father passed away.

Her mind went back to that day eight winters before when she had stood in the library of their town house in Grosvenor Square waiting for a bridegroom, whom she had thought was the height of a maiden's dreams. It hadn't taken long to discover how mistaken she had been. When after the ceremony he had disappeared without a word to her, she had determined to make him sorry for ever committing such a breach of etiquette. Now her time of waiting was ended. In a month's time her bridegroom would be in London, and Nell had determined to be in residence waiting for him.

She turned to her companion and said, "Now, Benny, you know you have never failed me, dearest. You do understand, don't you?"

Miss Benbridge sighed deeply. Having a long acquaintance with the young woman, first as governess then companion, she knew it to be virtually impossible to change her mind. "I suppose I do, dearest. Are you certain you are doing the correct thing? I consider it my duty to tell you that you may not find his lordship as easy to bring to heel as you seem to think."

"It is not necessary to bring his lordship to heel, Benny" she said, disappointed to be put to the necessity of making explanations. "I am his wife. I am the Countess of Melford and I mean to take my place in society. He has no right to deprive me of that after eight years of marriage! You will agree with me on this point, I hope."

15

Miss Benbridge sighed again, knowing that it was no earthly use trying to talk to Nell when she was in this mood. "I suppose I must, dearest." she agreed at last.

"Thank you dearest Benny! Now we must turn our attention to our wardrobes. Oh, how exciting to be going to town again after such a long stay in the country! It will be wonderful to select a new wardrobe after a year in these dull garments." She lifted the edge of her full skirt and disgustedly allowed it to drop.

Refusing to pack more than a handful of her mourning garments, she politely informed Benny that she had no intention of hauling those black rags to the metropolis with her. A letter was sent off to the lawyer, telling him to open Melford House, and in little more than a week they managed to set off early one morning, to leave the quiet of the country behind.

Nell stared out the window for a long time watching the last of her beloved Devonshire as the trees and hedges moved swiftly past. For the first time she was taking up her rightful position, and she wasn't afraid of that, having been reared with all the respect shown to the daughter of a duke; but she felt that her old life was now truly behind her for the first time since that farce of a marriage eight years ago when she had been an innocent child of sixteen.

Accustoming herself to the bumping and jolting of the chaise as it bounced along, she let her mind go back to that Christmas vacation all those years ago when her father had announced that he had planned her marriage with the son of his old friend, Lord Melford. She had stupidly believed she had grown up at last. How soon she had discovered her mistake! Her bridegroom had disappeared within minutes of the ceremony, and the next week she had suffered the ignominy of being returned to Miss Simpson's select academy for young ladies. No one had ever known that she had been married during the winter break, and later Miss Benbridge was brought back as her companion when she left school. What a far cry from the substance of her dreams, she thought bitterly. Such a farce!

It was necessary to spend only one night on the road, so they weren't inconvenienced in the least, although on the second day of traveling Benny was quite fatigued as they entered London very late in the afternoon. The chaise slowed and made the turn into the gates at Melford House, and for the first time Nell felt apprehension. Barton, Lord Melford's man of business, had done his work well, however, and the liveried butler who opened the door to them welcomed the ladies with an eager smile. If he was a trifle surprised to hear that his lordship had married, it caused no concern as it had been expected for many years.

Nell entered the great hall without any betrayal of her apprehension that she would not be welcomed as was her due. She handed her muff to the butler, who in turn placed it into the hands of the first footman, saying all the while, "I hope you had a very pleasant journey, milady. Ah . . . my name is Welby and I am your butler." he informed her briskly.

.Nell smiled warmly at Welby, who was obviously an old family retainer and had most likely known his lordship in his youth and decided to take an open approach. "Thank you, Welby The journey was comfortable. Lord Melford has not arrived before us, I hope?" Her brows rose a bit.

"No, no, milady," he assured her hastily. "You are in plenty of time to plan an appropriate welcome for his lordship, if I may be so familiar." He permitted himself a small smile.

"Very good. Now, if you will be so kind as to show us to our rooms, Miss Benbridge, I am certain, will thank you. We will not come down for dinner this evening, but will have something on a tray in our rooms. I thought it unwise to bring my maid with me, as I felt it would be necessary to hire someone more suitable here in town. So if you please, send someone to assist me, and also Miss Benbridge." She favored him with a smile that won his heart, and he led the way up the stairs with his head very high, his dignity very much in evidence.

When they reached her suite, she turned to Benny, said, "Good night, dearest Benny. I shall join you at breakfast," and entered her room with aplomb. She stopped inside the door to stare at the opulent surroundings. Everything had been kept in perfect order she could see as she walked forward to drop her gloves and reticule on a chair.

The room had been done in shades of green; it was very pleasing, thought Nell, as she walked about first touching the canopy then a brocaded chair. The heavy draperies had been drawn against the night air, and with a sigh she kicked off her traveling boots and waited for the arrival of the maid she could hear in the corridor.

The next days passed in a whirl as Nell and Miss Benbridge rushed about madly repairing the damage to her wardrobe and making the acquaintance of various members of the ton who had been friends of her father. Nell had no apprehension that she would not be acceptable to the ton. One entire day was filled with visiting a fashionable modiste, who was able to supply her with the latest fashions, though it was tiresome having to stand for so long in one position while being fitted. Nell was particular to take only the best garments, for she meant to make her own fashion. It was fortunate that the prevailing mode for highwaisted gowns suited her to a nicety. She bought morning gowns of the palest greens to match her eyes, and a lovely lemon color that brought out the beautiful copper tones of her hair. Afternoon dresses, morning dresses, ball gowns, she had them all. Everything a lady of fashion might conceivably require, she purchased. As she had been blessed with a large allowance, money was no object and she pandered to her every whim for the first time in her life, though she was careful to make no mention of her marriage in her dealings with the ton or the tradespeople.

Two mornings before Lord Melford's return, Nell decided to go out for a few items she had missed between her other business. She had gotten to know the staff and met her servants, whose hearts she had won immediately with her gentle manner. As she and Miss Benbridge were leaving Madame Lisette's dress shop, Nell mistook her footing and plunged toward the ground, only to be caught in the nick of time by a gentleman who happened to be passing at the moment. Quite embarrassed, she flushed to the roots of her hair as she took her packages into shaky hands. The incident was over in a flash, and soon the gentleman had passed down the street in company of some friends, but Nell was haunted by his likeness. She

sternly tried to compose her shattered nerves by re-
minding herself she was a married woman and had
no right to allow herself to be so discommoded by a
passing stranger. She and Benny strolled on to the
corner, where her coachman was waiting patiently.
And try as she would, she could not banish the image
of the gentleman from her mind. The memory of his
dark eyes and the strength of his arms kept haunting
her as she struggled to remember where she had seen
them last.

Chapter Two

Andrew Merriweather, Lord Melford, strolled down St. James in a lighthearted mood. It had been eight years since he had been in London and he meant to reacquaint himself with the town immediately. It would be a very different thing now, he thought cynically as he remembered his earlier days on the town. With pockets usually to let he had spent more time outrunning the duns than he had enjoying the usual delights of the metropolis. That would be all changed now, he thought happily. After an extended stay in the Far East he had come home with his pockets in much better condition than when he had begun his journey all those long years ago.

Only one thing blighted his homecoming. He had been shocked to receive the news that his father and brother had been killed in a boating accident. He had not been informed of the details, but he suddenly found himself with the responsibility of the estate and it weighed heavily on his shoulders. He and

Lucien had been close, and only time would repair the sense of loss he felt.

Another thing nagged at his mind as he remembered that he had been married to a schoolgirl on the eve of his departure. He could barely remember the details of that day long ago, but he knew he had been wed to the daughter of a friend of his father's. *What was her name?*

Ah, well, he thought fatalistically. Possibly it could be annulled, he considered vaguely before dismissing his bride from his mind. The allure of London called him. Thinking to visit his clubs before going home, he sent his coach and baggage before him to Melford House. He enjoyed the unaccustomed sounds of the hustle and bustle of the city and barely noticed a gentleman of medium height who walked past, then paused to call out, "Andy? By heaven, it is Andrew Merriweather!"

Lord Melford stopped and turned about to discover who was hailing him. A happy smile erased the sad memories and he exclaimed, "Harry Claymore! Gad, but it has been a long time!"

The two gentlemen shook hands and slapped each other on the back, before strolling on together, and Harry brought Andrew up to date on all the latest news. As they passed a well-known modiste, two ladies stepped out with their arms filled with newly purchased packages. Suddenly one of the ladies tripped on her skirts, and Melford found himself holding a slim, fragrant bundle of womanhood in his arms. He just glimpsed a pair of flashing emerald eyes and a fiery blush before releasing her to stand on her own feet once more. He and Harry helped the

22

ladies retrieve their packages, then passed on down the street with a polite lifting of hats.

The two gentlemen retired to Boodle's, where they ordered a glass of wine and proceeded to catch up on their respective histories. Andrew told him as much as he knew of the accident that had catapulted him into the inheritance, and Harry listened intently.

Sir Harry said, "I am really sorry about your father and brother, Andy. I know you must feel it. The news was all over town, you know. It really was quite a shock. Lucien was well liked, you know."

"Thank you, Harry. I am forced to admit that the news set me back a pace. I never expected to come into the earldom, I can assure you," he said seriously before tipping his glass to empty it.

He shrugged off the nostalgic feelings about to engulf him and asked casually, "Did you know the young lady we met back there in the street?"

Harry reluctantly shook his fair head. "As sorry as I can be, old boy, but it is impossible. Never seen the girl before, but I wouldn't worry if I was you. Now that you have come home with a full purse and a title in your pocket, the matchmaking mamas will pursue you with the full forces at their disposal, believe me."

Andrew would not be distracted. "I am certain I have seen the girl before somewhere," he persisted. "I wonder where it can have been?"

Harry grinned. "Don't bother your head with it, Andrew. You can easily discover her direction, for she was obviously a lady of quality. Someone will know where she can be found."

Andrew smiled sheepishly. "I did not say that I wanted to see her again, bucko. No need to rush things. I am content as I am for the moment." He sat back to enjoy the remainder of the evening, renewing many of his acquaintances who were members of the club.

As a result of his conviviality it was quite late when his lordship was admitted to his home. As his baggage was admitted earlier in the day, Welby was waiting anxiously to receive him. When he strolled into the foyer at dawn, his cravat was askew and his clothing slightly crumpled from his imbibing too much wine and the hours spent at the gaming tables. His step was still quite steady and only one who was well acquainted with him could have known that his lordship was in his cups.

At sight of Welby, who had known him since he had been in leading strings, Lord Melford gave him a warm smile and clapped him on the shoulder. "How're you, Welby, old boy? It has been a long time, hasn't it."

Quite overcome, Welby answered, "It is a great pleasure to have you home once more, my lord." He paused for a moment, then said, "On behalf of the staff I would like to say how sorry we were to hear about his lordship and Master Lucien. It was very unsettling, sir."

Andrew handed him his cape, hat, and cane before answering, "Thank you very much Welby. I am going to miss them both." Then he ran up the stairs to the room that had been his father's. A feeling of nostalgia struck him forcefully, but he shrugged it off, and undressing swiftly he lay in the big comfortable bed and was soon asleep.

An early riser, Nell arose betimes the next morning to take her mare out for a canter in the park. It was fairly empty on this fall morning, and she let her loose to gallop freely for a time before turning to home to make the last preparations for Lord Melford's arrival.

She entered the tree-lined avenue and cantered to the mounting block, where she dismounted speedily, ignoring the helping hand of the groom who was waiting for her. Casting him a gleeful smile, she rushed up the steps and entered the house. She was ascending the staircase from the main hallway when a gentleman came out of a room on the next floor and started to descend. It took her only another moment to realize that it was the gentleman who had rescued her from a serious fall on the previous morning. A slight blush appeared on her cheeks, but she was preparing to question him severely when he spoke to her angrily.

"Who admitted you to this house, young woman?" he asked with his brows raised threateningly. "This is a private house, and I have no notion of what you may be doing here."

Nell had formed the intention of speaking civilly, but with these unbearable sentences she lost her temper completely. With green eyes flashing brilliantly she said stiffly, "I was about to ask you the same question, sir. I can assure you that I have every right to be in this house. Now, if you please, you may go away and leave me to enjoy my breakfast." Without another word she prepared to ascend the steps in his wake.

His arm shot out and grabbed hers with such force that she gasped. "Release me, sir, on the instant," she demanded. "I have asked you to leave. I am sure you would not like me to call my servants!"

"You seem very sure of yourself, my fine lady, but it won't work. I am the master in this house, and I say you don't belong here." He said angrily, enjoying the look of uncertainty that crossed her face.

Nell glanced about to assure herself that she really was in her own home and then said, "For a moment you had me believing that I had entered the wrong house by mistake. However, it is not so. This is Melford House and I have every right to be here. So, please release me at once," she demanded, pulling at his clinging hand.

His steely grip relaxed slightly while he searched her features for some sign of her identity. He said, "I don't know who you may be, but you are certainly correct. This is Melford House, and I am Lord Melford. So, you see, I have found you out. *Now,* will you leave quietly?"

Where her face had been red before, it was now deadly white. But, this lasted only for a moment and she regained her composure completely. He was not to know how the knowledge of his identity had shaken her placidity. With a shake of her bright curls, she said, "No, I won't leave quietly." Then she enlightened him. "I intend to have my breakfast, my lord. I hope you will join me." Enjoying the vexed look on his face, she added mischievously, "I believe you will agree that I have every right to share your table, my lord. You see . . ." She hesitated for a moment, then said, "I am *Lady* Melford."

Nell enjoyed the sensation her words produced. If the marble stairway had split open and landed them both on the cold earth outside, he could not have been more surprised. His mouth flew open for a moment, then he closed it and gulped before saying,

"Impossible! The girl I married was only a child. You could not possibly be she!"

"My lord, I don't intend to remain on the stairs discussing our private concerns for the benefit of the servants. If you wish, you may join me for breakfast. Otherwise . . ." She hesitated and began to climb the stairs again.

Without another word, Lord Melford followed her into the breakfast parlor. No words were exchanged during the meal, of which both husband and wife partook freely. When it was finished, Lord Melford rose and said, "I would greatly appreciate it if you would join me in the library, my lady."

When they were seated in the library, a comfortable room done in crimson shades, his lordship turned to Nell and said, "How does it come about that you are living here in my house? I was under the impression that you were still with your father."

Nell's face hardened. If she had not already been angry with him, this statement would have caused considerable fury within her breast. "I am living in your house, my lord, for the simple reason that this is where I choose to be. It has doubtless escaped your memory, but we *have* been married for eight years. When your lawyers informed me that you were returning home at last, I decided that it was time for us to set up house together."

"Oh, you did, did you?" He shot the words at her menacingly. "Well, let me inform you, ma'am, that I am not accustomed to having my life ordered for me by some slip of a schoolgirl. It might not suit me to be married to *you* or *anyone else at this time.*"

At this cut Nell's bosom rose. With a flashing eye she said, "Oh, *really?* Then you may hear this, Lord

Melford. I am not greatly interested in whether it *suits* you to be married or not. You *are* and *have* been married to *me* for the past eight years. I mean to set myself up and enter society, and you are going to help me. It may interest you to know that due to my marriage it was deemed unnecessary for me to have the usual coming out and presentation most young ladies receive. I obeyed my father in his lifetime, but since he is dead, and has been for the last twelve months, I have done as I please. I intend to continue doing so," she informed him firmly.

Lord Melford stared at her for a long moment without speaking. His first inclination was to give the chit the worst tongue-lashing of her life, but something held him back. It was true that due to his marriage with her she had been denied much that would have been her due. It behooved him to get some answers to some questions.

He cleared his throat and said, "It seems that I have been remiss in my duty to you. I recall very little about our marriage ceremony, but I seem to remember that you are called Elinor."

Nell smiled at him, pleased with his more reasonable attitude and said, "I was formerly Lady Mary Elinor Russell, daughter of the Duke of Devbridge. My friends call me Nell."

Seated at the desk, his lordship fiddled with a pen and looked at her steadily. "Very well, then. Nell it shall be. You may call me Andrew. It seems that we shall be married after all. How old were you when we were married?" he threw in suddenly.

Nell stared at him in surprise. "I was sixteen, Andrew. Why do you ask?"

"Because I had no idea you were so old. I thought

28

you a mere child if I thought anything about it at all. The only thing on my mind was the voyage I was beginning the next morning. If my father hadn't insisted, I would never have gone through with such a farce."

Nell shuddered, remembering the wedding. "You can't imagine how I felt. I was home for my break when my father broke the news to me. Somewhat naturally I obeyed his commands. I usually obeyed my father."

"What did you do after the wedding?"

"When I realized that I wouldn't be forced to deal with an ardent bridegroom, I was relieved. I was only sixteen and I felt terribly humiliated when his grace sent me back to school."

"What? You went back to school?" he asked in surprise.

"Yes. Miss Simpson's select academy for young ladies. After the initial humiliation was over, I was able to feel immeasureably superior when the other girls were speculating about their futures. I knew that mine was all set."

He roared with laughter. "You never told anyone?"

Nell's brows rose again. "Are you mad? I would never have breathed one word of our connection. Not even to Fanny Armstrong, and she was my bosom bow." She paused. "Besides, no one would have believed me." She looked a trifle cast down at this admission.

He laughed again as he considered this aspect of her plight. "No doubt. I suppose you have been with your father until his death. When did that take place?"

"Yes, I was. He passed away more than a year ago. When my cousin took over the estate, his rather large family so filled the castle that with his permission I took over the dower house. I brought back my own old governess to be my companion, and she has been with me since." After a moment she said, "I am sorry about the tragic loss you suffered, also, my lord."

A shadow passed over his face and was gone in a moment. "I thank you, Nell" he said. "It came as quite a surprise, but let us discuss something else. What cannot be changed must be lived with, don't you think?" He smiled warmly and Nell could not help but respond.

Pulling himself together, he continued. "It seems I have been remiss in my duties. I make you my apologies," he said brusquely. "Now, about this woman you have with you . . . She is still with you?"

Nell nodded. "She refused to allow me to travel alone, and she was not at all certain you would accept me when I arrived."

Lord Melford thought for a moment then said, "You may dismiss the woman if you wish. I think it would also be wise for me to take you to visit my great-aunt. That is where I was bound when we met earlier. It appears that I will have more to tell her than I ever dreamed. I wonder if father ever told her about our marriage? Aunt Melinda will help us, she will know just how to go about it to stop tongues from wagging. Now, run up and get your bonnet and we will call on her immediately."

Nell hurried from the room. She was glad to have her ordeal over. It had worried her more than she had cared to let on to Benny. She gave a sigh of pure relief. She decided to take a moment to give the news to Benny, and ran her to earth in the little parlor at the back of the house.

"Dearest Benny," she called out. "I have only a moment, but I am come to tell you that Lord Melford has arrived early, and I have had a long talk with him. Everything is all right, and you can retire to your cottage. I must run, but I'll tell you everything later. Good-bye!" She ran out the door and down the stairs to the hall where his lordship was impatiently waiting.

"I'm sorry to keep you waiting, my lord, but I really felt I should tell Miss Benbridge that I was going out. She has been very good to me, you see." Lord Melford took her hand to assist her to enter the coach, before seating himself beside her. When they were moving, she risked a glance at him and was totally disconcerted to find him looking at her. She flushed and stared at her clasped hands.

After a moment she said, "I wondered why I didn't know you when we met yesterday. You have changed in the last years, my lord." she told him shyly.

"Possibly," he said indifferently. Then with a smile and a flick of her auburn curls he added, "And so have you, my dear. I would never have known you for the child you were at that time."

"I should hope so!" she cried fervently. "I would hate to think I had remained the gawky schoolgirl I was then!" she said firmly.

"You may reassure yourself on that head, my dear. The ugly duckling has blossomed forth into a swan." He chuckled at her ready blush.

Before she could formulate a reply, the coach rolled to a stop and the footman opened the door to allow them to descend. Nell placed her hand in Lord Melford's outstretched hand and was annoyed to discover that her heart was beating shamefully fast. Looking up at him, she found him staring searchingly at her as if trying to summon the answer to some question that happened to be bothering him.

Chapter Three

Lady Rochdale sat quietly while Lord and Lady Melford told their story. To tell the truth, she was delighted and amused by it all. Not for a long time had she listened to such an amusing tale, and she determined to help the young couple out of their difficulty. It was obvious that they needed some help, and she was more than willing to give it. My, what an outcry there would be when it was bruited abroad that the rich Lord Melford had been snapped up by a chit from the country, and she not even presented!

Sitting in her parlor with a fat pug at her feet, she epitomized the foremost in fashionable women of the day, and she frightened Nell a bit. At last she said, "It seems to me, Andrew, that you have managed to get yourself into something of a pickle. I shall extricate you." This was said in something of the grand manner, and irritated Melford extremely.

Affronted by her words he said, "I beg your pardon, ma'am, but I don't see how you can accuse us of getting ourselves into a pickle. This pie was not of our making."

"You're quite right as usual, dearest, but you must still be extricated from this situation. Now listen to me while I expound." She turned to Nell with a smile. "The first thing you must do is be married. We can have a private wedding at home, then a large reception following to present you to the ton. I can't think why those two old codgers didn't do the thing right all those years ago."

Nell ventured to remark, "But we are already married, my lady. I don't quite understand."

Lord Melford added, "Nell is perfectly right, Aunt Melinda. I don't see the need for another ceremony. One was quite enough, thank you."

Lady Rochdale's black eyes flashed down at them. "I can see you are a pair of ninnies. First, if we are to put this thing over on the ton, we must make it good. It will be impossible to give it out that you were married all those years ago. That is to stir up the sort of scandal broth we are trying to avoid."

Lord Melford stood at the wide open window watching the passing carriages. His back was to the room and he threw over his shoulder, "For my part, the ton can think anything it deuced well wants."

"No doubt," the dowager said imperiously. "I am certain your bride will not agree with you. If you remember correctly, the purpose of this discussion is to discover the means of presenting Nell with all circumspection to the ton." Lady Rochdale regarded her nephew and his bride silently for a moment before continuing. "Are you ready to entertain my suggestions?"

Nell and Andrew stared at each other for a moment, then he shrugged and said, "We're in your hands, Aunt. What would you have us do?"

Lady Rochdale settled her gray wig on her head and said condescendingly, with the complacency of old age, "I knew you would come around, Andrew. You were the nicest little boy, excepting a few minor incidents," she said generously, neglecting to mention that the few minor incidents involved, for one thing, gluing the skirts of the vicar's obese wife to the pew one Sunday morning.

"Now, I shall issue invitations to certain members of the ton who can be counted on to attend the reception, which will take place one week from today." She turned to Nell. "I don't suppose you brought your wedding dress with you?" When Nell shook her head, she went on, "We must have one made up at once."

She turned to Melford. "Andrew, I just want to mention how saddened I was by that tragedy. I know you must feel it deeply." She changed the subject again and said, "Take a wedding trip or something and come back in the spring when all the ton is in residence and we will make your introduction properly."

The ride back to Melford House was a quiet one. Nell was in a snit and refused to converse. She had been looking forward to the little season and it seemed hard to be forced to another dose of the country. The couple parted at the door of Melford House, Lady Nell to the privacy of her suite, and Lord Melford to his club. It had suddenly occurred to him that it might be a good idea to warn Harry of his newly wedded state before he blabbed things all over town. He finally ran him to earth at Boodle's, after looking in at White's, Manton's Shooting Gallery, and Jackson's Boxing Saloon.

It appeared that he was already celebrating, for he had a glass of wine in his hand and a bottle sitting on the table. Melford seated himself near Harry and said with a grin, "Starting rather early, aren't you, Harry?"

Harry grinned and said, "The only cure for a hangover is a glass of wine. Works every time." He offered the bottle to Andrew, and called for another glass from a passing waiter.

Lord Melford pushed the bottle away and said, "Listen, Harry, I have something to tell you." He plunged into his story. It took some time, but in the end Harry sat back with his eyes opened wide and the wine forgotten. When he recovered his speech, he asked, "Who is the bride?"

For the first time during the recital of his story, Lord Andrew grinned boyishly. "You will never believe it, Harry. Do you remember the young woman we met yesterday morning? You know, the one who fell into my arms as we passed that dress shop."

"Of all the lucky fools! You're wed to a beauty, Andrew. Some people have all the luck!" Harry exclaimed in disgust and tossed off another glass of wine.

At the moment, the beauty being discussed was pacing the floor of her bedroom angrily. It had been her firm intention to remain in town, and she refused to have her plans thwarted. She would find a way.

The next few days flew past on wings. The dowager took her in hand the next morning after their visit, and the plans for the small wedding and reception went forward rapidly. Lady Rochdale kept her so busy that she never saw her husband more than a few moments a day, if one discounted the time spent at dinner. When the morning of her debut arrived—she could hardly call it anything else—Lady Nell knew no more about her husband than she had known the day he arrived.

The wedding was to take place in the library at Melford House, and the reception was to be held later in the ballroom. Not a full-scale ball, milady decreed, just a pleasant gathering. Musicians were hired, so there would be dancing, of course.

With all the necessary cleaning for entertainment on such a large scale, the house was a veritable beehive, and Lord Melford absented himself for the most part.

As all the clocks struck the hour precisely at seven o'clock, Sir Henry Claymore knocked on Lady Nell's chamber door. The maid informed her that her escort was waiting, and she went to meet him. Nell had been introduced hastily to Lord Claymore on the previous morning between the various shopping expeditions the dowager had planned.

Lady Nell smiled tremulously at Sir Henry as she placed her hand on his crooked arm. "Good evening, Sir Henry. How do you do?"

He looked down at her, dressed in her bridal finery and smiled warmly. "Wonderfully, my lady. May I say that you are in very good looks this evening?"

"Why, thank you, Sir Henry," she said as they proceeded down the main staircase, which was brilliantly lit in anticipation of the celebration that would soon be in progress.

They reached the library, where Lord Melford waited with the vicar, Lady Rochdale, and Miss Benbridge. The assembled company looked up as one, as Welby opened the door for Lady Nell to enter on Sir Henry's arm. Had Nell happened to glance at her bridegroom, she would have known that her many hours of wondering and longing had been wasted, for an expression of the warmest regard was in his eyes as they rested upon his wife when she entered the library in her white garments.

Sir Henry handed her into Lord Melford's keeping, and the wedding began. Nell was beautiful in the candlelit room. Her auburn hair gave her a warm, colorful appearance as she stood to make her vows to this man for the second time. Her voice was pleasantly low, though perfectly audible, and her hand trembled ever so slightly when she placed it into the strong one of her husband's.

Lord Melford was not noticeably nervous, but he was feeling ever so slightly squeamish. This wedding was not at all like his other one, and he felt apprehensive. When Nell came into the room looking so confoundedly lovely, everything else flew from his mind, leaving him as vulnerable as a schoolboy. He made his vows firmly, and was surprised to find that it was over so quickly. When it was time to seal his vows, he lifted the gauzy veil slowly and looked down into her face for a long moment. He wanted to impress her image upon his memory. Then his lips were upon hers in a warm tender kiss that blotted everything from both of their minds for a long, long moment. His arms slipped around her, drawing her tightly into his embrace, and Nell clung to his shoulders as she surrendered to the sweetness of his kiss.

When at length he released her, she continued to cling to him for a moment before letting him go. An

38

uncomfortable hush settled over the small group, and Lady Rochdale stepped into the breach.

"Congratulations, Lady Melford. I hope you both will be very happy, my lord." She turned to the vicar and said, "We have just enough time for the toasts before our guests arrive."

The vicar assented, and Lady Rochdale had Sir Henry pour drinks for everyone. When they had each been served, she said, "To your long and happy marriage."

"To a long and happy marriage," echoed the vicar.

"To your marriage, Andrew," added Sir Henry as he raised his glass.

Lord Andrew looked down into the flushed face of his wife and whispered into her ear, "To our long and happy marriage, my dear."

Nell colored up even more when she heard his words, but refused to lower her eyes from his, and agreed, "To our long and happy marriage."

They all drank the good health of the bride and groom, and for a moment nothing could be heard but the sound of good champagne being sipped in response to the various toasts. As they were finishing, the first carriages could be heard drawing up in front of the stoop, so the dowager insisted that they take their places in the hall. Nell greeted each one with a smile as Lady Rochdale presented them first to her, then to his lordship. After a while the faces became a blur and the smile seemed glued to her aching lips. Eventually, though, everyone had been greeted, and they were permitted to take their places in anticipation of the first dance, for which the orchestra was tuning up. The dowager had decreed a waltz for the presentation dance, although it was still considered to be slightly fast. Nell enjoyed the dance and was surprised to find that her husband was quite good at it, too.

They made a handsome couple as they circled the ballroom. His black head inclined toward the fiery curls that rioted beneath his chin. Andrew looked into her eyes, and caught his breath at the shimmering quality present in the wide emerald eyes that stared so trustingly back at him. His arm tightened instinctively about her as they swung into the final strains of the lilting waltz.

When the music stopped, Andrew brought her to a standstill near where Harry was in conversation with a petite blonde, who was talking quickly and waving her hands in explanation. The girl glanced up as Nell and Lord Melford came to a stop near them, and gasped in surprise and pleasure. She cried out, "Nell! It really is you! I thought I must be mistaken when we were introduced earlier. You didn't seem to know me."

Still feeling breathless after her dance with her husband, Nell said slowly, "Why, Fanny! I can scarcely believe my eyes. Did I snub you earlier? I don't remember," Nell asked with obvious pleasure, grasping her friend's hands in a fond gesture.

She turned to Melford with a warm smile and said, "My lord, allow me to make known to you a very dear friend of my girlhood, Fanny Armstrong. Fanny, the Earl of Melford."

A slight laugh erupted from the fair-haired bundle standing near them as Fanny said, "No longer Miss Armstrong, dearest. I have been wed to Lord Brockheath these two years past. And I am happy to meet you, my lord." She turned her eyes to Melford's face.

Although Melford said all that was proper, he took the first opportunity of removing Nell from her presence. He didn't like the look of shock that had appeared on her face when she had learned of her friend's marriage. It brought home to him as nothing could have done the rigors of her former situation. He remained at her side throughout the evening, devoting himself to her pleasure. The evening passed pleasantly, as laughter and conversation buzzed about them, and Nell enjoyed a first taste of the pleasure of being accepted into the society of her peers.

Chapter Four

When the evening was over, Nell, tired from the unaccustomed lateness of the hour, ascended the stairs with Lord Andrew beside her. Suddenly apprehensive, she glanced surreptitiously at him as they walked toward their chambers. She could perceive nothing by studying his manner, so with a mental resolve, she shrugged off her fears and went bravely to meet her fate. In any event, her fears were groundless, for when they paused outside her room, Lord Melford merely took her hand and with a practiced gesture kissed the inside of her wrist, saying, "Remember to rise early in the morning, my love. We should get off to an early start."

Nell was rather surprised, but grateful nonetheless, and so spoke to him in a much warmer tone than was her intention. "Good night, my lord. It has been an enjoyable evening. And I will *try* to be up betimes in the morning, sir."

He grinned and flicked aside a falling curl.

"Wretch," he said. "See you do," and he left her standing alone in the great hallway.

Nell stepped inside her sitting room and closed the door with a sigh. She realized that she was spending entirely too much of her time thinking about her Earl. Something would have to be done about that, she told herself fiercely. He hadn't made any move to bring their relationship to a more intimate footing, and Nell was grateful for his seeming lack of interest, for she hadn't quite forgiven him for abandoning her for so many years. The convenient marriage was a product of the times and not at all uncommon. Nell knew this, but gave a long sigh for all the romantic dreams of her childhood.

Nell allowed the little maid Welby had procured for her to remove her jewelry and replace it in the cases lying on the dressing table. Then she undressed slowly. It was not until she was sitting on the side of her bed giving her hair a last few strokes that she realized that her maid had put her into a sheer negligee of palest gold. Unable to refrain, a light laugh tinkled out as she realized what the woman had been thinking. Everyone thought she was preparing for her anxious groom to come to her room. How surprised everyone would be if they knew the truth of the situation.

Nell placed the engraved brush, a gift from her father, on the night table, and snuffed out the candle before climbing between the sheets for the night. A gentle smile was on her face, and she slept almost immediately. Things had worked out much better than she had dared hope, she thought dreamily as she drifted off to sleep.

Nell woke early the next morning, feeling wonderfully refreshed. She rang for hot water and made her preparations for the day. When the maid entered she said, "Such a lovely morning, I believe I will go for a ride. Send to the stables for me and have my mare brought round. I will be ready in thirty minutes."

The girl curtseyed respectfully, but said timidly, "But, milady, are you not leaving this morning? His lordship . . ."

Nell interrupted her with an airy reply. "No, no, girl. The plans have been changed. Please replace my things in the wardrobe. I won't be traveling today. Now do hurry."

A frightened look was in her eyes, but the girl curtseyed again and ran to do her bidding. Half an hour later, Nell ran down the steps of the town house and said gaily to the groom who was holding the bridle, "It is a beautiful morning. I can hardly wait to get to the park." She let him help her mount, then waited while he got into the saddle before leading the way into the street.

Her mare had become accustomed to the city traffic during the last weeks, and Nell felt a little bubble of excitement swelling inside her. She resolutely put aside any thoughts of Melford and his possible reaction to this start and enjoyed every moment of her ride in the crisp fall air.

There was very little traffic so early in the morning, and on her return journey she was taking one last boisterous gallop down the bridle path when she looked up to see Melford bearing down upon her. From his black countenance she knew she was in for a bad time. He said nothing to her at first, but dismissed the groom with a wave of his hand and waited until he was out of sight. Then he brought his mount around to her side and asked angrily, "What are you doing here, my lady? Have you forgotten our plans for the journey down to Melford Chase?"

Nell brought the mare to a proper trot and said serenely, "I have not forgotten your plans, my lord."

His exasperation was plain to be seen. "If you have not forgotten, I can only assume that for some reason known only to yourself you mean to anger me. If you will be so good as to explain, we can resolve the situation and be on our way."

His high-handedness only served to set up her back, and she merely lifted her chin and disdained to give an answer, keeping her eyes straight ahead.

He waited a moment, then tried again. "Dash it all, Nell, have I offended you in some way in which I am not aware? What the devil is the matter with you?"

At that, Nell looked at him and said gently, "You have not offended me intentionally, I suppose. However, I may as well tell you now as later that I don't mean to be bundled off to the country. I have had my fill of rural life, and I am not going back for some time to come."

He stared at her incredulously and said, "What a pity you forgot to mention that little item until all our plans were made!"

Nell lifted her chin. "I would have said something, but I felt that you would not change your mind. I believe in action rather than words. If you wish to go on to the Chase, you may do so. I know you have certain duties to perform and I don't mean to be a charge on you. Don't feel that you have to worry over me."

Now she felt the full force of his anger. "Why, you

45

sly little minx! I ought to turn you over my knee for this behavior. All the time so innocent! I don't believe you ever had the intention of leaving the city." He paused to catch his breath before continuing. "I am taking you home, and then we will leave later than I had planned. It will throw us behind, but that cannot be helped."

Nell shook her head and reiterated, "I am not leaving, Andrew. You may do as you please, but I am not going. I have friends in town, and I am certain I will find amusements to keep me occupied."

By this time they had reached home, and Nell silently allowed him to help her dismount before rushing up the stairs into the hall. He followed her in an instant and caught her arm to guide her into the library, with a muttered aside over his shoulder for tea and biscuits to be brought. When the door closed behind them, he released her and said, "Now, I mean to get to the bottom of this. Why don't you want to go down to the Chase with me?"

Nell paced casually around the room before taking a seat as far as possible from his position near the mantelpiece. "I spent the past eight years in the country," she said, "and I am sick to the core of it. I came to town with the intention of making a place for myself in society, and that is what I mean to do." She stared innocently at him. Before he could reply, the servant entered with the tea, and he had to wait until the tray was placed in front of Nell.

When the maid had gone, he said, "I can understand your feelings, Nell, but you agreed that it would be best for all of us if we waited until the spring for your presentation."

Nell shook her head in denial as she handed him

his teacup. "I never agreed to any such thing. No one bothered to ask my opinion. Between you and Lady Rochdale you settled the whole matter."

He was taken aback for the moment when he realized the truth of her words. "I am truly sorry, Nell," he said. "I had not considered your feelings on this matter." He paused. "Do you feel so strongly about remaining in town?"

Nell felt a pang of guilt at her behavior, but said, "Truly I do, Andrew. I couldn't be tied down in the country again so soon."

He set his cup down with a snap. "Then that settles it. We will remain in town for the present. However, I do have one request for you." His eyes twinkled mischievously and he said, "Do try to refrain from escapades like the one this morning. It is not at all proper to gallop so in the park." Nell flushed, but he continued. "And another thing, I can't imagine what any normal member of the ton might have thought had they chanced to observe you this morning, particularly in light of your being married last evening!"

Nell smiled ruefully. "Now that I think of it, I am sure I must have appeared slightly singular. I will try to reform, my lord."

When society realized that the earl and countess were in town, the cards came in abundance, and soon it became necessary for her to send her regrets for lack of time to attend all the functions. Accompanied by Lady Rochdale, who had forgiven her for ignoring her advice, she made a round of morning calls and soon was on nearly every guest list. She was found to be witty, charming, and beautiful. The ruling members of the ton found her worthy to be part

47

of their select society. She was pronounced to be a lovely young woman, not too pushing, who did not hold herself arrogantly although by birth and marriage she was among the foremost personages in the land.

Word soon spread that she was the fashion, and soon no entertainment was complete without the lovely young countess in attendance. The hour of promenade saw her always in the park, usually escorted by some handsome gentleman. Melford began to feel that he might never be alone again with his wife, for it seemed there was always some gentleman escorting Nell for a ride to some place or another. Nell renewed her friendship with Lady Brockheath, and soon the ladies were as close as ever they had been during the days of their youth. It was Lady Brockheath who introduced Nell to Viscount Lynman. He was present at a dinner party she was hostessing, one that Nell had attended alone. Melford had pressing business elsewhere.

Nell noticed the gentleman almost as soon as she entered the drawing room, for he was the only person present she had not met. His handsome good looks intrigued her, and when she was presented, she greeted him warmly. Fanny brought him across the room and said, "Viscount, I want you to meet a very dear friend of mine."

"Ah, yes, the beauty who just came in. I would be delighted," he said.

Lady Brockheath continued, "This is my very dear friend, the Countess of Melford. Nell, let me present you to Viscount Lynman. I am certain you will become great friends."

The viscount bowed gracefully and lifted her

fingers to his lips in an experienced manner. "I am delighted to be allowed to share the company of such a charming lady," he said.

Nell released her fingers from his strong grip and said, "I am pleased to meet you, I'm sure." When the company went in to dinner, he remained at her side, and it happened that he was seated on her left. They continued their conversation, Lynman keeping her engrossed throughout the meal. Nell was impressed with his charm and good looks, and she thought about him long after the evening ended.

After a few weeks in town something began to bother Nell. She heard whispered comments about her marriage, for the jealous and spiteful always managed to comment within her hearing. She heard talk of an old scandal concerning Melford and wondered what it could be. She decided to nose about a bit.

With this in mind, Nell called on Lady Rochdale one afternoon. If anyone in town knew the story, her ladyship was the one. The servant showed her into the morning room, where Lady Rochdale sat in state each day. Nell greeted the lady happily, for she had grown truly fond of her. After the polite amenities were over and they were settled with their tea, Nell decided her only course was to come out openly with it.

She began tentatively. "I have heard some very strange stories, ma'am, and I hoped you could settle some questions in my mind."

Lady Rochdale was immediately concerned. "What is troubling you, child?" she asked.

Nell found it hard to explain. After a moment she

49

blurted it out. "I have heard some strange rumors about Melford and I wanted to discover the truth."

Lady Rochdale nodded wisely. She too had heard the talk of that old scandal. "I suppose some busybody has been whining about that old affair."

Nell's ears perked up. *What old affair?* "Yes. Was Melford involved in a duel all those years ago? I can hardly credit it."

The older woman looked at her with a wise smile. "Don't fret about something that was before your time, child. I will tell you the truth, although I wouldn't mention it to Andrew." She drew a deep breath and began her story. "Andrew was a wild youth. He was an engaging scamp, but he was in trouble more than he was out. Unfortunately he became involved with an older woman whose husband took exception to the affair. There was no duel, although one was rumored. This little affair came on top of several smaller scandals, and the former earl came down hard on Andrew. He sent him out of the country to let the talk die down, and it must have about this time that your marriage took place."

Nell nodded blankly. "It was the day before he left."

Lady Rochdale patted her hand comfortingly. "Well, my dear, don't take this too hard. Andrew seems to have settled down nicely with you, and I haven't apprehensions for him. I advise you to ignore the gabblemongers and be happy."

Nell thanked her ladyship for relieving her curiosity, then made her way home to dwell on what she had learned. It is said that a little knowlege is dangerous, and so it was for Nell. She knew the barest facts of the affair, and it merely served to make her suspicious of her husband. She began to take an interest in his friends and noticed especially the females he was with at each gathering they attended together. As a result, she defiantly flirted and soon drew Melford's attention to her own behavior.

One evening she was feeling especially wild. Nell had accidentally met Melford riding in the park with a lovely young widow who was endowed with a colorful reputation. The story Nell had heard from Lady Rochdale came back to haunt her. *Was he reverting to his former behavior?* Nell asked herself nervously. It was doubly injurious to her feelings when she realized that he had paid her no more attention than was expected to convince the world that they had a normal marriage!

That night she came down the stairs dressed for the occasion. A ball was being held at Lady Jersey's home, and Nell was armed and ready for any contretemps that might arise during the course of the evening. Melford was waiting courteously in the drawing room when she came inside, and he welcomed her with a smile. Nell was especially beautiful in a ball gown of emerald satin that brought out the fiery glints in her eyes.

Melford lifted her fingers to his lips and said, "You are dazzling, my dear. You shall certainly shine tonight."

Nell curtseyed properly and said, "I thank you, milord. I might say the same for yourself."

An uncomfortable silence fell between them and then Melford said, "I believe I hear the carriage outside. Shall we go?"

Nell agreed and gathered her wrap, and took her ivory painted fan in her hand along with her reticule.

She allowed him to lead her to the carriage. When they reached the street where Lady Jersey lived, the carriage moved much more slowly. It seemed that everyone wanted to be fashionably late, which caused a crush in the square. Nell kept her eyes on the coach windows, for she had a faint, uneasy feeling in Melford's presence. His eyes rested on her slender form, and she could not quite read the message he was sending her.

When the carriage ground to a halt, the footman let down the steps and Melford descended first, then turned to help Nell. They went up the stairs and immediately were caught in the throng waiting to be announced. Lady Jersey received them cordially, shaking hands with Melford, then saying, "Countess, how delightful to receive you this evening."

Nell murmured something polite and passed into the room on Melford's arm. The dancing had already begun, and Nell looked around expectantly.

Sir Henry Claymore appeared miraculously and complimented Nell with a sigh. "Lovely Lady. No more beauty can be found in all England."

Nell grinned openly and said, "Come, come, Sir Harry. Spanish coin?"

He smiled at her and said, "Of course not, my lady. It is the truth." He offered his arm and said, "May I have this dance, ma'am?"

During this interlude Melford watched with jaded eyes but refused to comment, even when Nell turned to him inquiringly. When he made no objection, Nell placed her hand on Sir Harry's arm and curtseyed to her husband. Then she let Sir Harry lead her onto the dance floor. Although she kept up a running conversation with Harry, part of her mind was with Melford, who she noted did not hesitate in finding a charming partner to take her place. She could hardly help noticing that it was the same blonde widow he had been with in the park on an earlier occasion.

Once Harry noticed the direction of her eyes and asked, "Who is the beauty with Andrew?"

Nell shrugged her shoulders indifferently. "I am not certain. His latest flirt, I must suppose. Andrea Fairley, I believe. *Lady* Andrea Fairley."

Harry stared at her with all knowing eyes and asked, "Jealous?"

"Jealous!" Nell cried with a squeak. "Why should I be jealous?"

He laughed heartily. "It was just a thought, ma'am. Nothing more."

Nell sniffed and refused to reply. Their dance came to an end, and she found that she did not lack for partners. After a cotillion with an exuberant young man, she found that a flounce on her gown had come unstitched and excused herself to find a maid to repair it. As she was unfamiliar with the house, Nell found herself entering the library unexpectedly.

The room was occupied, and not intending to intrude she had started to back out as quickly as she had entered when the sound of Melford's voice stopped her completely. Nell took a closer look at the room's occupants and found to her displeasure that Melford and Lady Fairley were standing close together at the far end of the room, and it appeared Melford's arm was around her.

Melford was saying, "My dear Andrea, do not upset yourself. Everything will work out. I promise you."

Nell could not hear Lady Fairley's reply but retreated as silently as she had entered in silent astonishment. She found a maid, who made swift repairs to her gown, and returned to the ballroom without giving any sign that she had suffered a shock.

During an intermission, Nell found Fanny Brockheath, and they conversed quietly for a moment. While they were talking, Viscount Lynman appeared at Nell's elbow and bowed gracefully.

"Good evening, Lady Brockheath, Lady Melford. Good fortune has smiled on me at last, giving me the company of two such lovely ladies."

Lady Brockheath simpered and Nell smiled a welcome. He kissed their fingers in turn before saying to Nell, "I hope your card is not filled, my lady, for it would give me immense pleasure to have your hand for the waltz just beginning."

Nell looked up into his good-looking face and was disarmed. She placed her hand in his outstretched one and allowed him to lead her onto the floor.

She felt enormously shy for the moment, then he said, "I wonder if something is amiss with my neckcloth? Confound that man of mine!"

Nell glanced at him inquiringly before saying, "You jest, my lord?"

He laughed. "Now that I have your attention, my lady. I was sure something was amiss, you kept your eyes on it so determinedly."

Nell's laugh floated across the room to where Melford was standing with Lady Fairley. He glanced up casually to see his wife dancing in apparent enjoyment in the arms of the one man in all England he wanted to avoid. With narrowed eyes he stared at the graceful couple, who appeared oblivious of the crowd about them, and a searing anger moved through his body. He murmured an excuse, to the surprise of Lady Fairley, and stalked across the room to startle Nell, who was gazing at her partner.

Nell was moving along on a wonderful cloud of flattery, and she was enjoying it very much. After her surprising discovery of Melford and Lady Fairley earlier in the evening, his words fell on attentive ears. Although not forgotten, Melford had been pushed to the back of her mind. He had shown so little interest in her comings and goings that it was with stunning surprise that she found his hand on her arm, interrupting the dance.

He was perfectly courteous, but his intentions were clear. "You will permit me to cut in, Viscount? I must share this waltz with my wife."

Nell was at first stunned by his words, then shocked by the expression in his eyes. His arm when it encircled her waist was hard as a rock and filled with tension. The viscount bowed with an enigmatic expression in his eyes and made his way off the floor.

When Nell regained her powers of speech, she burst out, "What was the purpose of that, milord?"

His eyes were hard as he looked down at her and said, "I have reasons for not desiring that connection, madam. I pray you to remember."

Affronted, Nell lowered her eyes and turned her attention to the steps of the dance. She refused to speak further, and when the music ended she allowed him to lead her off the floor without comment. Another partner appeared to rescue her from her discomfiture, leaving her little time to ponder Melford's unusual words and behavior.

The evening dragged on, and although Nell appeared to be unconcerned by Melford's strictures, she was angered. Her eyes returned continually to him, and she noticed that he maintained a running conversation with the widow. When the supper hour came, she happened to be near Sir Harry, who offered his arm and asked to be her escort. Somehow, Melford managed to appear nearby with Lady Fairley on his arm, and together the two couples found their places in the dining room. They sat at a small table for four, and Nell was supremely uncomfortable. For the first time she made the acquaintance of the lady, who she was forced to admit was a lovely creature and quite guileless. Melford informed them that he had been acquainted with Lord Fairley since his early days on the town. Sir Harry, too, had known the gentleman, and Nell was left feeling like an outsider as the three of them discussed old times.

When the supper hour ended, Nell found herself escorted by Melford, Harry having hustled Lady Fairley off at the first opportunity. Nell looked up at her husband and said bluntly, "I am sorry you are left with me on your hands." She looked about and spied Lady Rochdale on the dais with the dowagers and added, "If you will be so kind as to take me to Lady Rochdale, I won't trouble you further."

She felt his arm tense at her side. "What gave you the notion that you were a trouble to me, madam?" he asked. His voice was harsh, and more than anything Nell wanted to escape his presence. When she refused to answer, he said, "Well? I am waiting for an answer."

Nell swallowed nervously. His behavior had been a puzzle from the outset of the evening, and she hardly knew how to answer. "Well, I did promise not to be a bother to you," she stammered, "and not interfere with you in any way." She ended nervously.

He glared at her for a moment before saying, "Have your wits gone begging, Nell? I haven't the faintest notion what you are babbling about. Try for a little sense."

Nell suddenly became aware that they were causing a spectacle and said, "I have the headache. Please take me home."

Melford became aware of the sensation they were causing and led her to their hostess, where they made a speedy good-bye. When they were finally seated in their carriage, Melford again raised the question. "I believe you have something to say to me, madam?" he prompted.

By this time Nell had gathered her scattered wits and answered, "I meant nothing more than I told you. I don't mean to force myself on you more than is necessary. I am perfectly conversant with your feelings toward this marriage, and I don't mean to make the situation more difficult than necessary."

Lord Melford was at a momentary loss for words as he realized for the first time what Nell's feelings and position had been. He said, "I beg you not to think of it. When you are intruding upon my privacy, I shall assuredly alert you. This brings me to another matter, ma'am. I don't know who introduced you to Viscount Lynman, but let me assure you that that is a connection I don't mean to harbor. You will keep your distance."

Nell *had* been feeling very docile, but her former temper returned at these words. She was a high-spirited girl, to say the least, and to give her a direct order was like waving a red scarf at a bull. She charged. "I have no intention of keeping my distance from Lynman. If he should happen to call, I shall be at home," she said airily.

He grasped her wrist in a bruising grip and said, "I think not."

Nell managed to shrug carelessly and said, "We shall see."

When the carriage stopped, she jumped down without giving him time to assist her and ran into the house. She did not stop running until she reached her chamber.

During the next few days, Nell and the Earl met only at mealtimes, their engagements being in different quarters of the city, but one afternoon Nell passed him in the park with Lady Fairley beside him and knew what he had been doing during his frequent absences. Bitterly angry, she determined to renew her acquaintance with Lynman at the first opportunity. That came sooner than she expected. A chance meeting during a morning of shopping gave her the opportunity she needed. Soon Lynman was escorting her regularly and their names were linked closely after the scene she had shared with Melford on the evening of the ball.

Although she was still angry with Melford for his behavior, it was not entirely to spite him that she continued her flirtation with Lynman. He was a charming rogue and flattered her with continuous compliments. Nell truly enjoyed his company. She heard the whispers but ignored them all, except for one story she heard connecting him to the scandal Melford had been involved in many years ago. Nell was agog to hear the end of it, but she could discover no one who knew the whole story and was forced to be satisfied with speculation.

Preoccupied with his own affairs, Melford had no idea that Nell had carried out her threat to continue seeing the viscount. Finally Harry informed him one evening at the club. Andrew was on the brink of leaving when Harry appeared and asked, "Could I have a word with you in private, Andy? Won't take a moment."

When they were seated over a bottle of wine, Harry seemed strangely reluctant to speak, and Andrew said, "You wanted to talk to me?"

Harry smiled weakly and answered, "Yes, I do. The thing is that it is not easy to say what I have to say."

Melford's brows rose. "I can't imagine anything being that troublesome. Have a go at it."

"It is about Lady Nell, Andrew." He hesitated for Andrew's brow had blackened. "It must have escaped your notice that she has been causing quite a story in town with Lynman."

"I had no idea," Andrew said. "When did this happen?"

Exasperated, Harry asked, "Where have you been, man? Nell has been seen at nearly every important function under his escort. I had thought you would object, but it seems that I . . . If I am intruding, old boy, don't hesitate to tell me so."

Melford's eyes were hard as he answered, "It seems I must take stronger measures." He sighed and added, "I have business at the Chase. It will have to be rustication, I suppose. Nell won't like that." He rose from the table. "I will say good-bye for now, Harry. Thank you for telling me."

Harry watched with troubled eyes as Melford made his way from the club. He toasted him silently before drinking deeply from the glass.

Chapter Five

When Melford left White's after his conversation with Sir Harry, he went home immediately, his first inclination being to confront Nell at once. But after due consideration he decided that in this instance subterfuge would serve better than directness. Accordingly he called in his butler and Nell's maid and gave instructions for their immediate removal to the Chase.

He deemed it wiser to inform Nell only at the last moment, for he had not forgotten her earlier reaction to his plans to remove from society. He grimly made his plans, then kept out of her way for the remainder of the afternoon. Indeed, he was not the best of company, for the discovery of her association with Viscount Lynman had brought old memories to the surface, and they came back in a painful rush.

Lynman and Andrew had never been the best of friends during their youthful acquaintance, but their tolerance for one another had turned to profound dislike when they found themselves in rivalry for the favors of the lovely Lady St. Clair. He grimaced bitterly as he reconsidered the folly of his youthful actions. Although Andrew had certainly been foolish and hotheaded, it was the viscount who had caused the scandal. When Lady St. Clair preferred the attentions of Andrew, Lynman had been determined to have his revenge for his rejection.

Lynman informed St. Clair of the plans Andrew had made with Lady St. Clair, and it was only the veriest good fortune that Harry Claymore had happened to overhear their conversation in time to warn them. Andrew had left the house only moments before St. Clair's return.

The story was whispered about all over town, and his father had turned nasty. In retrospect, Andrew was grateful for the quick thinking of his father, who had ordered him from the country and almost certainly saved him from disaster. His father had not known it, but India had suited him down to the ground, and armed with letters of introduction he soon had access to foreign society. His marriage had troubled him not at all during his first years in the East and he had had affairs with more than one willing beauty.

It was unfortunate that after several years in the East, he should come upon Viscount Lynman in an out-of-the-way town. Andrew was not at all surprised to discover him attempting the seduction of a young girl of good birth, and was forced to intervene. This time their meeting had ended in a duel in which Andrew pinked him neatly.

Their ways had parted soon after, and Andrew had not laid eyes on Lynman since that time. It was with considerable distaste that he thought of him escorting his wife, and he meant to see that it did not happen again. Andrew hadn't the faintest notion of how fervently his distaste was reciprocated. Lynman now had two marks against Andrew and his hatred knew no bounds. This time he would even the score!

Having no desire to meet Nell before their departure, Melford took dinner at his club, leaving her to dine in lonely splendor at home. Nell had no particular objection to his desertion of her, for it was not at all an unusual occurrence. She had no notion of what was planned for her, but decided to remain in and have a quiet evening alone.

Next morning, as was her custom, she dressed in her habit and gave orders for her mount to be brought round. When she came downstairs, she was surprised to find Melford waiting for her in the hall. He looked up and said, "I hope you won't object if I come along with you?"

Nell shrugged and said, "You may do as you please, my lord."

Andrew took this churlishness in stride and said, "Shall we go for a drive in the curricle, Nell? I believe you would enjoy it."

Nell was suspicious of his motives, but acquiesced with a shrug. "Why not? It could be enjoyable," she said before leading the way down the steps.

Melford handed her into the curricle before climbing up beside her. He took the reins and guided the horses slowly into the quietness of the early morning street. He took the main road through the city, and suddenly Nell became suspicious. She clung to his arm and asked, "Where are we going, Melford? This is no mere morning ride!"

He glanced down at her imperturbably and said, "Unhand me, please, before we all land in the ditch!"

Nell glared at him angrily, but released his arm. "Where are we going, Melford? Are you kidnapping me?"

He laughed and said, "Impossible. How can a man kidnap his own wife?"

Furious, Nell cried, "I demand an explanation at once."

"You shall have an explanation, my dear. I have made arrangements to stop for breakfast at a posting house not too far distant. All will be made clear then."

Nell was speechless. She had not suspected for a moment that he was capable for such an action. She was impatient and was happy to see the posting house when it came in sight.

Melford helped her to descend and led the way into the inn. Nell followed angrily, hardly waiting for the door to close behind them in the private parlor Melford had bespoken before bursting out, "I want an explanation for this dastardly behavior, Melford."

He leaned nonchalantly against the mantelpiece and said, "After breakfast."

Nell allowed him to seat her at the table. "I couldn't swallow a morsel."

The servants had laid the table and the food was steaming. "Certainly you can. Have some of this ham."

"Ham? How can you suggest such a thing?"

"Very well, eat nothing," he said quietly, "but I insist on eating my breakfast in peace, so be quiet."

Nell was simmering but held her peace until he had finished his repast. She was even tempted by the smell of the food and ate a slice of bread and ham. When he was completely through and the servants had removed the last of the dishes, he said, "Now, we can discuss this unfortunate situation."

"I am happy you have found time to do so," she said sarcastically.

"Hard words will not make things better, Nell. I believe you will know what I mean to do when I say this. I told you not to make an intimate of Viscount Lynman and I meant it. Since you chose to disregard my request, I am placing him out of reach. When we return to town it is to be hoped that you will have learned some restraint."

A wave of humiliation and anger washed over Nell, and it was a moment before she could speak. Then she said, "How dare you take that tone with me? You have no right to treat me so!"

"I have the right to treat you any way I choose!" he shot back. "I will not have my wife an intimate of one of the worst rakes and blackguards it has been my misfortune to meet."

"How dare you say such a thing, you, you, philanderer!" she cried.

"I repeat. Hard words won't help the situation," he said with raised brow, although he was thinking, *philanderer? Why the devil did she say that?* "Now, shall we go?"

Nell rose from her seat and stalked out of the inn, only to be brought to an abrupt halt by the sight of the large traveling carriage with Melford's crest upon the door. She turned to Melford, who had followed her outside and said, "What is the meaning of this?"

65

"You will be much more comfortable in the chaise, Nell," he said bluntly.

Nell was obstinate. "I have no intention of entering this carriage, Melford," she said coldly.

His eyes gleamed angrily and Nell felt a shiver move down her spine, but she made no move to enter the chaise. "That is as you wish, my dear. However, should you put me to the necessity, I feel tolerably able to forcibly assist you to enter the chaise, and if you continue to stand here I will do so immediately."

Nell held her ground for a moment more, but soon realized that to continue would be an exercise in futility. She could see by his firm jawline that Melford would not change his mind. "Oh, very well," she said and entered the chaise with a flounce.

Nell looked about herself with distaste. The pink satin cushions and curtains were not at all to her liking, and she knew they clashed violently with her hair. As the morning wore on, she fumed and fussed as she considered Melford's audacity in bundling her willy-nilly out of town. She was furious that he should try to impose his will on her, especially as he had shown no interest in her well-being whatsoever.

Nell had ample time to consider her grievances, for Melford did not bother to look in on her from the time they left the inn until they stopped later in the day for a change of horses and a quick luncheon. Nell was determined to inform Melford of her exact opinion of his actions. With bosom swelling, she waited for her husband to hand her down from the chaise. The door was open, the steps let down, but Melford was not waiting to hand his lady down. One of the liveried grooms was holding his hand up to her, and this ignited her wrath once again.

66

Melford came out to meet her as she entered the inn, and with outstretched hand he said, "I rode on ahead to order our meal. I knew you would be famished and worn by the journey."

Nell had the feeling he was laughing at her, although not the faintest glimmer of a smile was on his face. She ignored his hand and said, "How very kind of you, my lord. I must strive to be properly grateful." With her head held high she stalked ahead of him into the dining parlor.

Melford stared after Nell in amusement, and said to himself, Now what ails the chit? He had hoped she would be recovered from her first spasm of anger. Ah, well . . . He was thoughtful as he followed her into the room.

Nell had not finished with him. She turned round as soon as he had closed the door and said, "I wonder if I might hope to be allowed to remove my bonnet and wash my hands before dining, my lord? Or is it too much to hope for?"

Lord Andrew sighed deeply and said, "I intended to have the landlord's wife show you up to the room I had prepared for you, but you didn't give me the opportunity to tell you, my dear."

This information should have soothed her lacerated sensibilities, but it did not have the desired effect. Instead of calming her it merely fanned the flames of her wrath. She picked his seemingly innocuous words to quarrel over. "And I am not your dear, Lord Melford. If you don't mind, I am going to my room."

Melford was fast losing his patience with the vexatious chit. Before she could stalk from the room in offended dignity, he halted her by grasping her shoulders and drawing her to a standstill. Her emerald eyes glared at him in anger, and for a moment he stared down at her intently. "Now, *my dear*," he said, "I want an explanation of this tantrum you seem intent on throwing."

His use of the word *tantrum* was unfortunate, for Nell had been softened by his momentarily tender expression. This hardened her heart again. "I am not throwing a tantrum, my lord. I have every reason to be upset." She spoke through gritted teeth. "Now, if you will release me, I will hurry to perform the necessary in the shortest possible time."

Although of very easygoing temperament, Lord Andrew could be a formidable enemy when aroused. Some of this temperament showed now, as he shook her slightly and said, "I hope you don't mean to keep me waiting for the remainder of the afternoon, Nell. I should have thought you would have accustomed yourself to the situation by now," he said sternly. "What has put you in alt?"

Nell shrugged and said airily, "Not a thing in the world, my lord. I hope I am not one to hold a grudge, but I do not make a practice of riding hours on end in a vastly uncomfortable chaise with nothing other than the cushions to talk with!" Now this was a blatantly false accusation. Although it could not be denied that she had been alone, the chaise was perfectly comfortable, and well sprung.

A wicked glimmer appeared in Lord Andrew's eyes and he said, "If it is company you want, then company you shall have. Now go upstairs."

Nell stalked from the room, her mind a jumble of accusations. Melford had no right bundling her out of town like so much baggage! And what was between him and the viscount? she asked herself. It was absolutely too much to credit, after his behavior with Lady Fairley! Nell continued to simmer and was very much upon her dignity when she entered the parlor sometime later.

When they finished their meal and recommenced their journey, Nell found that Melford meant to travel inside with her. "It is not at all necessary for you to put yourself out, my lord," she said. "I assure you I can while away the time perfectly well," she added acidly.

He refused to be baited, merely replying, "No doubt, my dear. However, I shall ride along with you all the same." His eyes twinkled at her, and once again Nell was certain he was laughing at her. "Had I known you disliked riding alone, I would have brought your mare. On our next journey I shall do so, weather permitting."

After a quiet moment while Nell wondered at his sudden change of front he said, "Would you care for cards? It would while away the time."

"Thank you, I should like that." What was the man up to now, she wondered anxiously.

While he brought out the cards and set up the board between them, he said, "Don't you think it is time you accustomed yourself to calling me by my given name, Nell? Make it Andrew in the future, or Andy if it pleases you."

Nell looked at him in puzzlement for a moment before saying, "I will try to remember, my lord." He grinned and admonished, "Andrew!"

An unwilling laugh broke from her and she whispered, "Andrew."

"That's better," he said, then dealt the cards. They

were quiet while they studied their hands, but it soon became apparent that he was the superior player.

When Nell tired of the game, she threw in her hand and said, "Tell me about your family, Andrew. Although our parents were good friends, my father never told me much about you, or your family." She grinned and added, "He did say that your father was bang up to the nines, but no more could I get out of him." She hoped to discover some clue to his hotheaded behavior all those years ago.

His laughter echoed hers. "That sounds very like something my father would have said. It is obvious why they were such good friends." Their joint laughter sounded loudly in the chaise. Then he continued, "As you know, my home is Melford Chase. There is not really much to tell. I haven't been to the Chase myself for eight years, so I can't tell you what condition it may be in." An apprehensive frown crossed his face for a moment before he said, "It should be well kept up, though, for my father was very well to pass." He was quiet. "Your father made a good settlement at the time of our marriage," he added uncomfortably.

Nell hesitated before commenting, "I don't know much about it. Father didn't choose to discuss finances with me at all. It wasn't until recently that I knew there had been a marriage settlement."

Melford stared at her in surprise. "I would have surely thought you informed, but it is possible." He surveyed her for a long moment. "Your extreme youth could have been the reason. One can't expect a child to understand such things," he added, unwittingly rekindling her anger.

"It appears to me that your wits have gone begging, my lord. If I was old enough to be married, then one can't accuse me of being a child. I assure you I would have understood well enough."

He grinned at the flame of color that had come into her cheeks. "Now don't get into a pelter, my dear. I assure you I don't still consider you a child. But, really, you know you were much too young to be married."

Nell opened her mouth to refute this statement but thought better of it. The memory of herself as she had been eight years past came before her eyes and, bitter though it was, she was forced to admit that his words were true. She bit her lip before replying ruefully, "Of course you are right. I would never submit a daughter of mine to such treatment, I assure you."

Before she knew what was happening, Lord Andrew had her encircled in his arms and was looking down at her in a very disturbing manner. "I am of the same mind, my dear. No daughter of yours or mine shall ever be submitted to such turkish treatment." His voice had deepened, and before she quite knew what he was about, his lips had fastened upon hers and all power of concentration had flown. A warmth spreading from her middle moved out to send a flush from the top of her head to her toes, and she clutched his shoulders tightly.

His arms tightened about her for a moment before he released her with a jerk. Nell replaced her bonnet, which had been pushed aside, and both were quiet for a time.

When they stopped at an inn for the night, Nell excused herself immediately, choosing to have a warm bath and a tray in her room. Nell thought long and hard about the day's events. Melford's behavior

71

was certainly puzzling, and Nell was forced to admit that she was more interested in her handsome husband than she had heretofore realized.

Melford was not sorry to see Nell go up to her room, for he was having a similar battle with himself. It was quite a shock to discover that he was inordinately fond of his longtime but little-known bride. He determined to get to know her better, and with this in mind he enjoyed his dinner while considering several modes of attack.

Having come to no clear conclusion about Melford's intentions with regard to herself, Nell came downstairs with an air of aloofness, while Melford was determined to be pleased at any cost. Nell conversed pleasantly on any subject he cared to name, but she maintained her distance and Melford was unable to get through to her.

Understandably piqued, Melford determined to force his bride to open up to him, and had no idea how hard it was for her to retain her resolution under the full force of his charm. His smile was so welcoming it was almost more than her life was worth to keep her resolution firm. She had not forgiven him for forcing her to leave town, but for now it was in the back of her mind.

When they were seated in the chaise on the final stage of their journey, Nell asked pleasantly, "How long will it take us to reach Melford Chase?"

Resting comfortably on his side of the chaise, Lord Melford propped his booted feet on the opposite seat and said with a yawn, "I surmise that we should arrive before luncheon, my dear." Then with a casual gesture he pulled his hat over his eyes and, beneath her scandalized gaze, went to sleep.

Now, it was one thing for Nell to ignore his lordship in an effort to teach him a lesson, but it was entirely another basket of fish when he retaliated in turn! She endured this callous treatment for as long as possible, then said, "My lord, I wish you would tell me about this country we are traveling through. I am certain it is familiar to you."

Her only answer was a sleepy grunt. He didn't even lift his hat to give her the satisfaction of seeing his dark eyes.

She tried again. "My lord, I don't like traveling alone. I wish you would sit up and talk with me."

He straightened for a moment then said, "What shall I tell you?"

"It would please me greatly if you would tell me more about your family, my lord. And it would also please me if I weren't obliged to talk to your hat," she added haughtily.

"I thought you had no interest in the countryside!" he said wickedly.

Nell continued as if he had not spoken. "I have been wondering about your family, my lord. Were you the only child? Have you no brothers or sisters other than Lucien?"

His face darkened for a moment, then he said, "There was only the two of us. My father remarried after I went away. Did you never hear about it?"

Nell shook her head slowly. "No, I never heard anything. My father lived secluded, and I never heard anything about his friends."

He sat up and dropped his feet to the floor of the chaise. "From what I hear there isn't much to know. The poor female died soon after the wedding, and I never heard from my father again. Actually, it was only when I heard from the lawyers that I learned of his remarriage. He died only recently, you know."

This information incensed Nell. "How outrageous. You should have been told of such a momentous event as your father's marriage. Why, it is monstrous, sir," she cried in agitation.

He covered her hand soothingly. "Don't fret for me, child. I assure you it did not upset me in the least. We weren't really close, and I hardly expected him to notify me of anything. I was busy making my own fortune. I know my father was taking care of my best interests when he arranged our marriage, and at the time no one could have known how things would come about. However, I am happy that I don't have to bear the standard of a fortune hunter," he said earnestly. "I only regret that my brother Lucien is not able to take my place. I had no desire to stand in my father's shoes."

"It would not have mattered," she told him earnestly, reflecting his serious tone. "And I am sorry about your father and brother. I wish I could have known them."

"Yes, it would have mattered, Nell. I don't think you would like to have such things bruited about. This way no one knows the truth of the matter. Besides . . ." He hesitated, then said, "I am making a large settlement on you as should have been done earlier." He ignored her reference to his family.

Taking a deep breath, Nell said shakily, "Andrew, no. You have no need to do that. You know my father left me sufficiently well provided for. You must not."

He squeezed her fingers and said stiffly, "It is most necessary. I believe I am sufficiently well blunted to

74

provide for my wife. It is all arranged with the lawyers."

Nell peeped at him under lowered lashes and realized that the matter was one that touched his masculinity. She refrained from saying more. "It is kind of you, Andrew, and I do thank you."

They fell silent and after a long time fell into desultory conversation. Soon Melford said, "Look about you, my dear, for we are on our own property." He pointed out the window. "If you will keep your eyes on that distant pinnacle, you will find that it turns into the house in a moment."

It was just as he told her. Sitting comfortably close together, they stared out the window in the direction of the house, Lord Melford anxious to see his home after a long absence and his bride eager to see her new home. When Nell saw the house for the first time, a gasp of pleasure escaped her. It was a stately building, constructed in the shape of an E with several separate wings, thus affording considerable privacy. A relieved smile appeared on Melford's face when he saw that his home had been kept in good condition and well cared for. He need not worry about that aspect of his long-neglected duties.

He leaned back with a sigh of relief, and only then did Nell feel the true extent of his previous anxiety. The coach rolled on around the bend and stopped in the courtyard in front of the house. To Nell's surprise, the entire staff was assembled before the door to greet them, and suddenly she was all aflutter. She clutched Melford's arm. "What are they doing there?" she asked.

He laughed. "It is an old custom. They always

turn out to greet the return of the master and mistress of the house. Come, you have nothing to fear."

He stepped out of the carriage and offered his hand to assist Nell. He led her to the head of the line of servants and introduced her to the butler, who remained stiffly on his dignity. Ceremoniously he bowed to Nell, then presented each of the servants in order of precedence. When he finished he dismissed the servants, although they did not all leave the vicinity but stood gaping while Melford greeted his old nurse with a great smile.

"Well, Master Andrew," his nurse said, "I am happy to see you home from them foreign parts. Why, it is a wonder you didn't starve to death." Andrew hardly minded her words, for he had long been acquainted with her opinion of foreigners.

"Now, Penny, don't fuss. You see me here before you in the heartiest good health," he chided. "Come and meet my bride." He pulled Nell forward.

Mrs. Pennybold curtseyed to Nell and looked her over boldly before saying, "Well, Master Andrew, I never thought to see you bring home such a right one. What with all them pranks before you went off. A real lady."

Nell hardly knew how to respond to such forthrightness, but Penny turned back to Melford and said with a misty smile, "We have missed you, my lord," thus rescuing Nell from formulating a reply.

Lord Melford laughed happily and placed a kiss on the old woman's cheek. "I don't believe it, Penny. Are you trying to put me in my place?"

She smiled at him and tapped him on the cheek with a wrinkled hand. "No more sauce from you, Master Andrew. I do know my place." She glanced around the crowded courtyard at the assembled servants and muttered, "As it seems some others do not!"

In a trice the yard was magically cleared and Melford was able to assist his bride up the steps unhindered. A new voice could be heard coming from inside the house. "Will you be so kind as to refrain from giving orders to the staff, Mrs. Pennybold? I do not feel in need of your services, I thank you."

"Don't think to be giving me any of your orders, Mr. Thimble, for I have no need of them," said Mrs. Pennybold with a sniff. She marched up the back stairs to leave Thimble waiting for his master in outraged dignity. His white hair was neatly in place and to Nell, as she entered the large, imposing hall, he looked every inch the old family retainer.

Andrew strode forward, tossing off his greatcoat and hat as he went. His voice was alive with pleasure. "Thimble, how are you, old chap?" His dark eyes lit up as he looked into the old man's happy face.

"Well, Master Andrew. Very well. I trust I see you in like manner? Did you have a comfortable journey?" he asked while looking curiously at the new bride.

"Quite well, thank you. I am never ill, you will remember, Thimble." He turned to Lady Nell with a smile and an outstretched hand "Nell, I want to present to you one of my earliest allies. Thimble was here before I was born and can tell you far more about Melford Chase than I can."

Lady Nell dimpled at him, causing him to fall under her spell immediately. "I am happy to meet you, Thimble. Perhaps you can tell me something of his lordship at a more convenient time?"

77

Thimble took her cloak and bonnet from her hands, and placed them into the hands of a waiting maid, saying, "I am sure I would be delighted, my lady, but for anything of that nature you should ask Mrs. Thimble, or Mrs. Pennybold. I am certain they can give you all the information you require." His eyes twinkled merrily, although his face remained set in impassive lines.

Melford grinned and said, "Don't try to ruin me in the eyes of my countess, Thimble. My crest will be considerably lowered if those two get hold of her. If you would have someone show my lady to her room, I want a word with you in the study," he added. "Oh, and bring me a bottle of Madeira."

As Thimble went to do his bidding, Melford turned to Nell with a grin and said, "Mrs. Thimble will show you to your rooms, my love. I'll join you later for luncheon. Shall we say in forty-five minutes?"

"I believe it can just be done," Nell told him with a smile, and was surprised when his arm went around her to draw her into a close embrace. Under the approving eyes of his servants, he placed a warm kiss on her lips. Then with a squeeze of her shoulders he added, "Until later."

Nell followed dumbly behind Mrs. Thimble, who bustled ahead of her in a businesslike manner toward a door at the end of the hall. Had Nell chosen to risk a glance over her shoulder, she would not have spent the next few moments in idle speculation, for while she was ascending the stairs, Melford stood silently watching with distinctly brooding eyes, until she disappeared.

Nell entered the master bedroom to find herself in

78

a room decorated in various shades of lemon brocade. The large bed dominated the room, covered with a yellow canopy and curtains. A small sitting area had been arranged near the wide windows with two chairs and a small sofa done in the French fashion in lemon and cream brocade. Nell smiled with satisfaction and said, "How lovely, Mrs. Thimble. Thank you so much for bringing me here."

The lady felt like chatting for a moment, and was anxious to show the room off to advantage. "I hope you find everything to your satisfaction, my lady. This is the master chamber, you know." She went to a door in the side wall and opened it saying, "This is Lord Melford's dressing room."

Nell followed her into the room, to find a smallish room elegantly furnished in the same yellow colors of the bedroom. A small daybed stood against one wall, along with a bureau, a shaving stand, and one comfortable chair. Her eyes rested for a moment on the small bed and her nerves immediately tensed. *What would he do? Would he? Did he mean to make their marriage a real one?* Nell abruptly moved back into her chamber and said, "I must change. It is nearly time for lunch."

After Mrs. Thimble had gone, Nell dropped nervously into a chair and awaited the arrival of her maid. It was all very odd, and she had no idea what Melford intended now. Shortly her maid entered and began unpacking her trunks that had arrived earlier. Nell could hear the servant moving about in Melford's dressing room and realized that his valet was taking care of his belongings.

Frowning thoughtfully, Nell undressed and poured water into the bowl to wash her face and arms. It was a pleasure to don a lovely afternoon gown with a pleasing quantity of lace and ruffles. Nell sat quietly while her maid brushed her hair, pulling it up high onto her head, then allowing one curl to fall over her shoulder, accenting the line of her slender neck where the gown fell away from her shoulders.

They were finishing the final touches of her brief toilet when a sharp knock was heard at the door. The maid opened it and Nell received a surprise. As if her thoughts had conjured him up, Melford entered from the door to his dressing room. "I want to talk to you, Nell," he said.

As it was the first time he had ever been in her room, she was confused, but gathering her wits Nell dismissed the maid and asked him to be seated. After a moment he said, "I wanted you to know that you may feel free to do as you choose with the house. You might like to meet our neighbors. There are several families in the neighborhood."

Nell thanked him politely but for the most part was silent in his presence. It was nearly time for lunch, and he rose and stood before the glass, making delicate repairs to his neckcloth, while Nell stared at his back in confusion. She was not at all accustomed to a gentleman making free with her room and was about to favor him with her opinion of his behavior when he turned about and saw the expression on her face. "You do not mind my using the mirror in *our* room, I hope, milady? You are aware that it *is* perfectly proper."

Totally confounded, Nell could only accept the arm he offered and allow him to escort her to luncheon with what dignity she could muster, ignoring the wickedly amused smile on his face. He had assuredly won that round, she thought wildly as they went into the dining parlor.

Chapter Six

The next few days went by in a flash for Lady Nell. Her mornings were spent with Mrs. Thimble, who seemed intent upon showing her the entire house from attics to cellars. Nell had discovered an unexpected urge to update the house and make it more fashionable. Melford had given her permission to make any changes she happened to fancy, and Nell was taking full advantage of his unexpected largesse.

Nell and Andrew were housed in one wing of the mansion, on the second floor, while the schoolroom was at the other end of the building. It had taken most of the first morning to view the lower floors, for Nell wished to look at everything in detail. She suddenly found that everything concerning Melford was of profound interest to her.

She found that though shabby the rooms were very well kept up, and it would take very little to bring everything into order again. Immediately, she sent off to London for some books and sample materials, and soon the house was buzzing with maids hired for the purpose of turning the house inside out in an effort to make it shine again.

To her surprise, Melford kept to himself for the most part, attending to his long neglected duties. He had taken up residence in his dressing room, relieving her fears that he meant to consummate their marriage. His volatile behavior disturbed her, and she hardly knew what he would do from one moment to another.

One afternoon he sent a message to her to meet him at the stables, and with great curiosity she obeyed. She could hardly imagine what he intended. He was pacing in the yard when she appeared, and a smile crossed his face when he caught sight of her.

He came to meet her with outstretched hands. "I have a surprise for you, Nell. Come and see."

The groom was just bringing Nell's mare from the stables, and Nell gasped with pleasure. She ran forward exclaiming, "Oh, you've brought Lady!" She patted the mare on the nose and said as she nuzzled her pocket, "Ahha, you greedy thing. I haven't any sugar for you today, my lovely."

Nell turned to Melford with a smile. "Thank you for bringing Lady to me. I have missed her."

He laughed. "I was certain you had, Nell. I remembered how often you rode when we were in town."

Nell looked at him in surprise, for she hadn't thought he had been aware of her comings and goings. He was a marvel, she thought anxiously.

Nell accompanied Melford into the study when they came back inside. He rang for wine, and she said, "I want to thank you again for sending for

Lady." She hesitated, then said, "I am sorry for causing such trouble for you. Perhaps we can be friends?" She offered her hand to him, but almost drew back at the last moment, for something she saw in his eyes disturbed her. When his hand touched hers, he continued to propel her forward until she was in his arms. He picked her up and moved to the big, comfortable armchair near the fireplace, where he sat down with her in his arms.

"Andrew, what are you doing?" she cried out, slightly frightened. Struggling within his embrace, she exclaimed, "Release me, Andrew! Thimble will return in a moment with the wine!"

He laughed and said, "Unless you want to start the gossip, you had best be silent. If not, you can continue to struggle. It is all one to me." His arms tightened around her. At that moment, the door opened, and Nell heard Thimble enter the study. He paused for a moment in surprise at the tableau before him, then imperturbably placed the tray on a table.

Nell felt a flush cover her features, and buried her face in Andrew's shoulder. She heard him say, "That will be all, Thimble. Thank you." She kept her face hidden until she heard the door close after him.

When at last she looked up, Andrew was grinning wickedly down into her embarrassed eyes. "Release me, Andrew," she begged. "Oh, you are insufferable!"

He laughed and said, "Why should I be, my lady? I feel that I have been sufficiently patient with you. You are my wife, you will recall!"

Nell gasped angrily as he took advantage of her emotional reaction to press his lips on her cheeks, then feather them across her eyes. When she moved

84

her head angrily, her lips accidentally touched his as he continued his embrace. He grasped her head in an iron grip and murmured against her lips, "I had no idea you were so eager for my kisses, my love. You shall not be disappointed."

Nell opened her mouth to tell him exactly what she thought about his kisses, when he swooped down and buried his mouth in hers. All sensible thought fled as time, space, and earth disappeared for them. To Nell it was like the moment of truth when the thing that had been puzzling her for so long all came together. She loved him! Suddenly she knew for certain. She loved him. Later she would think about what had happened to her, but for now it was enough to feel his warm lips pressing hers and feel his arms moving tighter and tighter about her body.

As suddenly as this revelation had come to her, she realized that she was no longer struggling within his embrace. Her arms were tightly clinging round his neck, and she could feel the softness of his dark hair in her fingers. She was furious with herself! She had meant to make him sorry for the years of neglect she had suffered, and now she was as weak as any schoolgirl, pining for his lovemaking.

When he released her momentarily, she said, "Let me go, Andrew. I don't want you to do this." He did not speak, for his lips were moving forcefully on hers again, desperately, urgently, bringing her dormant desires to the surface, making her forget her deepest resolve.

Nell pressed her face into his shoulder, and he stroked her hair gently, his arms still tightly around her. After a moment, she stirred and looked at him shyly. He grinned at her and said, "Silly, foolish

Nell. You insisted we maintain our marriage. It seems you did not take everything into consideration."

In a moment all her wrath resurfaced. "You certainly intend to take advantage of that, too. I am well aware of your intentions, my lord."

He stared at the flushed features, the tumbled rusty curls, and sighed. "So you think I should look elsewhere for my amusement? Is that what you really want, my dear? I could, you know."

Her eyes clouded, and for a painful moment she thought about Lady Fairley. Then she said painfully, "You may do as you please. I have no interest in your amusement, as you call it."

She tried to pull away, but his arms tightened again, and this time they were ruthless. "Your wishes don't matter in the least, my love. If I choose to have you, I will." His lips scorched her and she felt the heat welling up from deep inside her body. His hands moved over her, sending tiny chills to her extremities. This time when he released her, she stood up, her breast heaving.

"You have no right to use me so, my lord," she spat at him angrily. "If you dare to touch me again, I . . . I," she spluttered, trying to think of something, anything she could say. She finally managed, "I will shoot you," and fled the room, not stopping until she arrived in the master chamber.

The door slammed behind her as she entered the room, her cheeks flushed. Nell was furious with herself, Melford, her father, and the whole world. She railed against the fate that made him her husband and was angry that he had taunted her with the possibility of taking a mistress. How had he dared

86

say such a thing to her? He had no right to even think such a thing. If he dared to take a mistress, she *would* shoot him! Her mind in a turmoil, she failed to notice how illogical her thoughts were becoming. Pacing the floor, she worked herself into a fine fury. At last she heard him enter his dressing room in preparation for dinner and decided to follow his example.

Her maid came in response to her ring, and it took her half of her usual time to dress. Her fury had not subsided when she dismissed the maid. She stood looking down into the rose garden for a long interval, then heard a door open. Melford was standing in the room, dressed meticulously in his formal dinner rig. Plainness was now the vogue, and it became him mightily.

He looked her up and down and said, "I see you haven't recovered from your megrim."

Nell's eyes flashed. "I never suffer megrims, my lord."

"Then what is bothering you, my dear? You look positively vaporish."

Nell gasped and said, "I never had the vapors in my life. How dare you accuse me of such a thing?"

He shrugged disinterestedly. "Are you still in alt over our little discussion of this afternoon?"

"I am not in alt, sir. You must explain yourself, I believe." Nell was determined to be disagreeable.

"I meant every word of our conversation, Nell. I thought I would inform you of that before we went further. I also thought you might be interested to know that although I don't believe for a moment that you have the slightest knowledge of firearms, if you should decide to point any of them at me . . ."

Nell broke in on him. "I am an expert shot, my

87

lord, and if I should shoot at you, you may be very certain that I will hit my mark."

He shook his dark head and said, "I refuse to believe it. I have never yet seen a woman who could bear even the noise of a gun, much less . . ." He broke off as she interrupted him yet again.

"So you do not believe me, my lord?" Nell moved to a drawer in the little desk near the window and drew forth a small gold pistol. As his eyes fell upon it she said, "What do you say now, my fine lord?"

He held out his hand for it and she said, "I would handle it carefully if I were you, my lord. It happens to be loaded."

Lord Melford examined the gun for a moment, then said, "I don't believe you can fire this gun, Nell. I don't have the slightest notion what you may be doing with it, but . . ."

"I most assuredly can shoot it at any target you choose. Would you care to lay a little wager upon it?" Her eyes glowed with twin emerald fires, and Melford was a trifle surprised at this reaction.

"I will not wager with you upon such a subject for I know you could not possibly win. I am not in the habit of fleecing innocents." He laughed at her look of outrage.

Nell was so angry now that she was nearly beside herself. She took the gun from his hand and said, "Follow me." She stalked from the room without another word. Down the wide circular staircase she went and out a side door into the garden. Turning to Melford, who had followed her, she said, "Name any target you choose."

Melford watched her furious face, and was entranced by her loveliness. At last, hoping to humor his angry spouse, he pointed to a leaf hanging some few yards distant.

Nell looked at it and said, "Very well." She judged the distance expertly and in one swift move she turned to the side, raised her arm, and fired. The leaf fluttered to the ground. Now truly interested, Melford strode forward to retrieve the leaf. He picked it up and swore.

"Gad, but I've never seen such fine shooting, Nell. Where did you learn?" He walked back to join her with the leaf in his hand.

Nell stared at him angrily for a moment before saying, "My father taught me. I told you we lived secluded. There was nothing else to do." Then she added, seemingly unable to stop herself, "And if you insist upon flaunting your wretched mistress in my face, I certainly *will* shoot you!" She fled into the house, leaving Melford staring after her in astonishment.

His only coherent thought was, *What mistress?* He stared at the leaf in his hand, then at the door through which his wife had disappeared, and a smile appeared on his face. When he entered the dining room, the leaf had disappeared, but he was in spirits and was whistling.

Nell was appalled at her outburst in the garden and hardly had the nerve to go down to dinner, knowing it would surely be an intimate meal. She wondered if she would ever get through it. It was impossible to send down a message, for he would recognize it for what it was and force her to accompany him. She gathered the tatters of her dignity about her and entered the dining parlor with her head high. A surprise awaited her.

Melford was all courtesy as he looked up, his expression revealing no trace of their earlier contretemps when he spoke. "Ah, there you are, my dear. I feared you were ill." He carefully seated her at the table.

While he seated himself at the head of the table, she gave him a suspicious glance. Now what was he planning? "I needed to freshen up after our stroll in the garden," she told him for the benefit of the footmen.

"But of course. I should have known." His eyes twinkled merrily, but she couldn't fathom his thoughts.

Nell was beginning to feel the aftereffects of her tantrum and found it difficult to keep her countenance. How she had disgraced herself in his presence, she thought gloomily as she tasted the succulent morsels of meat that were on her plate. What next?

Melford had no intention of allowing her to ignore him. He kept up a light conversation throughout the meal, asking questions that required an answer. She was relieved when the meal ended and she was able to leave him to enjoy his port in solitary comfort.

Nell left the room a little dispiritedly and wandered through the empty rooms. When she found herself in the music room, she sat down at the pianoforte and allowed her fingers to run over the keys in a desultory manner. She played one waltz after another, but they could not seem to lift her spirits. Soon she retired for the night.

Melford maintained his friendly, aloof attitude during the next weeks, and Nell wondered constantly what he could be at. Several of the ladies and gentlemen in the parish came to call, and she was very pleased to receive them. In no time it was her turn to make return calls, and soon she was involved in a busy social life.

It suited Nell very well to be busy and out of the house, although it often became necessary for her and Melford to attend the same function. The hunting season was upon them, and the festivities surrounding the hunt kept the little community busy during the ensuing days.

Melford had invited a party of friends down for the occasion, and Nell was soon busy with preparations for their entertainment. Sitting in her morning room, a cup of tea on the table beside her, she considered the matter.

The gentlemen and some of the ladies would certainly be out with the hunt each morning, but other than that it would be up to Nell to provide entertainment.

Of course there would be a ball at the end of the hunt, but what else would be appropriate? Nell's brow wrinkled with worry. She decided to have a few couples in for dancing one evening and a small dinner party on another. Surely they would be able to amuse themselves for the remainder of the sennight, she thought wearily.

They would be arriving soon, and Nell perused the guest list slowly. Sir Charles and Lady Marlowe were family. Caroline Marlowe was Nell's cousin and it would be a relief to have her. Mr. and Mrs. Wardmont were friends of Melford's from the Far East. He had known them for several years and seemed to be fond of them. They were bringing their daughter, a young girl ready for her presentation, Miss Jane.

Lord and Lady Eversleigh were relatives of Melford, so she would have to be on her toes concerning her relationship with Melford. Nell sighed as she continued to read the list. Last but certainly not least was the young woman Melford had been friendly with in town. Lady Andrew Fairley. A young widow, it was said that she dominated any company she found herself with, and Nell was quite certain why she had been invited. She shrugged petulantly. If Melford wanted it that way, then so be it. She would not be responsible for the consequences. Unknown to Melford, she had done something to even up the numbers a bit. Sir Henry Claymore. Dear Harry! He would be a comfort to Nell in the days ahead. Let Melford dally with his widow. Nell would form an attachment of her own, then see how he liked it! Nell pondered her plans gleefully.

The following morning Nell arose betimes. She was determined to be about when the first guests arrived, and certainly it was not long before lunch when the carriages could be heard on the drive. Sir Charles and Lady Marlowe were the first arrivals and Nell greeted them happily, hugging Caroline tightly. As the two ladies embraced, she cried out, "Caroline, how good it is to have you with me again!"

Lady Marlowe, a lovely brunette, reciprocated fondly and said, "I'm so glad to see you looking so well, dearest." In her ear she whispered, "Not in an interesting situation, I see."

Nell flushed and said, "Hardly, Caroline." She turned and made the introductions, all the while conscious that Caroline's whisper hadn't been very discreet. From the wicked glint in Melford's eye, he had heard every word.

Soon the remainder of the guests had been greeted and shown to their respective chambers. It was nearly time for dinner when Nell was at last free to retire for a moment. She had just finished dressing when Melford knocked at the connecting door. Nell was sitting before the dressing table staring in the glass when he entered the room. She turned to give him a quick smile over her shoulder before turning back to the mirror. She was becoming accustomed to his intrusion in her room, and it no longer caused her embarrassment.

An air of recklessness, caused, no doubt, by the arrival of guests, was upon her and she smiled warmly and said, "We are very gay tonight, Andrew. Shall you enjoy the company?"

His long fingers rested on her bare shoulder and he smiled at her in return. "Of course, dear. I long to give you pleasure, as I am certain you are perfectly aware."

"You tease me, sir, I vow." Nell met his eyes in the glass for a fleeting moment. "Was there any particular reason for this visit?" she asked, fumbling with her brush as it lay on the table.

He stared down at her for a long moment, then said, "Yes, there is, my love. I wanted to inform you of something."

"So very serious, sir?" she asked with an attempt at flirtation. "I am certain you will spoil the party if you continue in this vein." She rattled on, needing to ease the sudden tension.

"No, no, my dearest. I intend to be the gayest of

the gay tonight. I have no intention of spoiling your party." He laughed at her expression.

"What did you wish to tell me?" she asked again. "Some weighty matter, I presume?"

"Again you wrong me, Nell. I merely wanted to inform you that I shall be sharing this chamber during the ensuing visit. I am certain it will be hard on you, but there it is."

Nell stared at him in surprise for a long moment before asking, "But why, Andrew? You have never . . . I mean . . ." She broke off in confusion. "Why should you wish to stay with me now?"

His eyes twinkled at her and he said, "Being well acquainted with your prowess with the pistols, I don't intend to be shot due to your overworked imagination."

Nell rose to face him and said with dignity, "It is not well done of you, sir, to remind me of words said in anger, and as quickly regretted. I do not believe the situation warrants such drastic measures," she said determinedly.

His smile was wicked, but he added virtuously, "I am merely taking a necessary precaution, my love. You cannot blame me."

She refused to reply. Indeed, she knew not what to say, and he intervened. "You're quite in looks tonight, Nell. I have something here for you. I think they will go well with that blue gown. He removed a jeweler's box from his pocket. Inside lay a sapphire necklace and earrings. He removed them and said, "Turn around and I will fasten them for you."

She felt the warmth of his fingers at her neck, and he said, "I have something else here, too." He placed a matching bracelet and ring on her right hand.

Tears were swimming in her eyes when she looked up at him at last, and with difficulty she said, "Thank you, Andrew. It is not at all necessary for you to give me jewelry."

He tilted her chin with a finger and told her firmly, "I give you jewelry for my own pleasure. It pleases me to see you happy, Nell." He dropped a quick kiss on her upturned lips before adding, "Put on your earrings, love."

Nell turned to the glass and placed the stones in her ears with trembling fingers. When she finished, she turned to him with a roguish smile and asked, "How do I look, Melford?"

He stared her up and down for a moment, then said, "Ravishing. Positively ravishing."

Impulsively, Nell threw her arms around his neck. Their lips met in a quick kiss and she whispered, "Thank you, Andrew."

His arms enfolded her and he answered, "If I had known a few trumpery baubles would affect you so, I would shower you with the confounded things."

Nell clasped her hands together behind his neck and said, "But perhaps you would not want me to live in your pocket, my lord."

"It might have its compensations," he said intriguingly, with a glint in his eyes.

They were a circumspect couple as they descended the main staircase later. The first of the guests were trickling downstairs, and Melford became involved in his duties as host. Nell was likewise employed.

The Wardmonts were present when Lord and Lady Melford entered, and though Nell liked Mr. Wardmont well enough, she couldn't help feeling that his wife was not at all what she had been accustomed to.

As is usual in such gatherings, the gentlemen somehow congregated, discussing the morrow's hunt, and the ladies were left to converse alone. Nell was surprised at her feelings for Lady Fairley. At this meeting Nell found that she liked her very well. The girl (Nell could scarcely call her a woman) looked no older than herself, and she didn't have the appearance her reputation had given her. If Melford had not shown an interest in her, as he obviously had by insisting that she be invited, Nell could have liked her very well. Her blonde curls cascaded over white shoulders, and her smile was open and friendly. A woman of indeterminate age was with her, and Nell was quick to recognize a paid companion, as she had been so recently plagued with one herself. Not that Benny had been a plague, and Nell hoped that she was happy with the cottage she had longed for, for so many years. Consequently, her smile was much more friendly than it might have been when she greeted Lady Fairley.

A friendly atmosphere remained in the room until Thimble announced dinner. Lord Melford offered his arm to Lady Eversleigh, his cousin, as the highest ranking lady, and he was followed by Lord Eversleigh with Mrs. Wardmont, Mr. Wardmont and Lady Marlowe, Sir Charles and Lady Fairley. Sir Harry gallantly offered both his arms to Miss Wardmont and Nell, who accepted it gladly.

The seating arrangements had posed some difficulty, but Nell fancied that she had settled them somewhat happily. It gave her a little consolation to know she had placed Lady Fairley as far from Melford as possible. It would have been intolerable to watch him pursue his flirtation at the dinner table each evening, and Nell swore not to endure it.

As the first course began, Sir Charles turned to Nell and asked with a pleasant smile on his face, "How is it that we have not been introduced previously, my lady? My Caroline speaks of you often."

Nell returned his smile and said, "I have lived secluded for the most part, Sir Charles. You knew that my father had recently died?" He nodded, taking a sip of his wine, and she continued. "When the mourning period ended, I was soon married. My husband has been out of the country for so long, it was deemed necessary that we retire to the estates for a period." She shrugged her dainty shoulders. "With one thing and another, you can see how it happened."

"It was certainly my loss, my lady, for whatever reason. May we hope to see you in town during the spring season?" he queried. His fair hair fell in waves from a center parting, and Nell found him hard to resist.

"I believe so, unless anything prevents," she responded shyly.

Realizing that she had been ignoring Sir Harry, she excused herself and turned to him with a rallying smile. "We were happy you could join us, Harry. I am certain Melford was excessively pleased to see you," she said with a glint in her green eyes.

"Of course," he agreed. "I must confess that your invitation pleased me well, for I had a lively curiosity as to how the newlyweds were coming along."

"Now that is naughty of you, Sir Harry." Her eyes

sent a message to his. "You of all persons must know the circumstance . . ."

"True," he agreed. "But come, confess. It is very like a play. One wonders what may come about next."

"I fear I must agree with you, Sir Harry. Alas, I also must await the final scenes of the script," she said with a laugh.

His laugh roared out over the dinner table conversation that had been kept at a polite social level, and Melford stared at them questioningly. Harry made some idle remark, and soon all the guests were involved with their own dinner partners.

However, the eyes that watched them took on new speculation, and each was wondering if the earl's new bride was taking on a lover so soon after the wedding.

When the meal ended, Nell rose with dignity to escort the ladies back to the parlor, where a lively conversation ensued. Hardly had the ladies seated themselves than Caroline rallied Nell. "I see you are upon terms with Sir Harry, my dear." She waggled a finger, and a mischievous smile was upon her face. "Best have a care, Melford won't take lightly that connection," she teased.

"Really, Caroline, such indelicacy. I vow, it is nothing," she answered, ready to indulge in a little foolish play. "Sir Harry is more to the taste of Lady Fairley," she teased.

"Such a handsome creature! I assure you, Lady Melford, you may present me at any time." Lady Fairley dimpled.

Miss Wardmont was astounded by such forwardness, and said with a wide-eyed look at Nell, "I

98

would never have thought you capable of such a flirtation, my lady."

Mrs. Wardmont began to remonstrate with her, but Nell silenced her with a look. "It is nothing, child. One accustoms oneself to the vagaries of polite conversation. It is nothing more, I assure you."

Miss Jane looked puzzled but refrained from any further comments, for which Nell was thankful. It could hardly be other than embarrassing if she persisted in making such remarks.

Much more teasing and chatter of this nature ensued. As a result, Nell was much in charity with Lady Fairley when the gentlemen entered the drawing room later in the evening.

Lady Eversleigh remained in conversation with Mrs. Wardmont, coldly ignoring Nell as far as possible; and Nell, realizing her feelings, was patently glad of it.

Mr. Wardmont mentioned something about piquet and soon a table was being set up at one end of the room. Melford, Mr. Wardmont, Lady Eversleigh, and Lady Fairley sat down to play. At another table Sir Charles, Lady Marlowe, Lord Eversleigh, and Mrs. Wardmont took their places. Unable to make up a third table, Nell invited Miss Wardmont to play for them on the pianoforte, and somehow she found herself sitting tête-à-tête with Sir Harry on the sofa.

Miss Wardmont was an accomplished player, and for a few moments they were lost in the beauty of the music. Then Harry turned to Nell and asked with a discomposing directness, "What has happened since you came down to the Chase, Lady Nell? I sense a coldness between you and Melford. But, no . . . that

99

is not quite what I mean to say. I can't really describe it."

Nell stared at him for a moment, feeling an urge to unburden herself to him, then said, "I have no earthly notion as to what you are referring. Melford and I are like most couples," she said with a shrug.

He shook his head and removed the fan from her trembling fingers. "That is not really so." He inclined his head toward the card table where Melford was partnering Lady Fairley. "There seems to be something, yet nothing at all. It is a great puzzle. I must put my mind to it."

Nell exclaimed unguardedly, "No. You must not!" then blushed. "I . . . I did not mean that, Harry." Gathering her dignity about her, she said, "I mean to say that you must not be concerned for us, Sir Harry. Melford and I will come about."

"So you *will* own that things are not what they should be," he persisted. "I could speak to Andrew, if you wish. Why was Lady Fairley invited, I wonder?" he mused aloud as he opened and closed her fan idly.

"Do not speak to Melford," Nell quietly urged. "I am capable of pulling my marriage together and need no help from you or anyone else," she ended.

They were interrupted by the arrival of the tea tray, for which Nell was grateful. She took her place behind it in a composed manner and dispensed the tea speedily. Harry persistently remained by her side, and she was beginning to feel the speculative stares of the other members of the party. Lady Nell could only be thankful when at last the other ladies showed unmistakable signs of wishing to retire.

When they went up for the night, the ladies were

seemingly drawn into separate groups. Lady Eversleigh and Mrs. Wardmont were in the former, and surprisingly, Lady Fairley, Lady Marlowe, and Lady Melford in the latter. Miss Jane seemed to be wavering between her mama's obvious disapproval and the relaxed friendliness of the other ladies.

After bidding the others goodnight, Nell retired to her chamber, where she hurriedly changed into her nightrail and dismissed her maid. She had much to think about. Nell had been so certain that Melford was inviting his mistress to the Chase, and yet ... She shook her head wearily. She could not believe such a thing of Lady Fairley. It was as Harry had stated. Things were puzzling, and she hardly knew *what* to think.

Nell got wearily into bed, forgetting that Melford had stated his intention of sharing it with her. It had been a long day. She pulled the covers up to her chin and turned on her side, letting her long flaming curls cascade out behind her. She slept.

Much later Melford entered the room, an evening of hard drinking behind him. The gentlemen had returned to cards after the ladies had retired, Lord Eversleigh being an ardent gambler. Weary also, Melford had spent a trying evening trying to keep the stakes down and was glad to take to his bed.

Candlelight fell across the covers, lighting Nell's hair, giving it the appearance of a flaming halo. She was sleeping so prettily, he feared he would wake her as he got into bed. What had she been thinking, he wondered, as she spent the evening in the company of his friend? Although engrossed in the cards, Melford had not missed a gesture the couple had made as they conversed on the sofa.

101

Sighing wearily, he pulled back the covers. He slept nearly as soon as his head touched the pillows.

Nell became aware of something heavy across her waist and a softness tickling her chin. As she wakened fully, she turned her head to discover that she was not alone in the great bed. Her heart pounded as she tried to recall the events of the preceding evening, but try as she might, she could not remember Melford joining her in bed. He must have come up much later. Of course, she had been unusually weary last evening. Nell gave up trying to think.

A groan sounded from the man lying so close to her, and his head nuzzled closer, then turned to face her, and he buried his face in her smooth shoulder.

Nell lay quietly, hoping he would not waken, but instead give her the chance to slip from his hold. It was a forlorn hope, for as soon as she made her first move, his arms tightened about her and she was forced to remain in his sleepy embrace.

Waiting for a moment, she said, "Please release me, my lord. I wish to rise."

His smothered chuckle tickled her soft skin, and she could feel the touch of his lips move across her shoulder. "Perhaps I don't want you to rise, milady," he said as his lips explored her shoulder fully, then continued upward to her neck and face.

Nell tried to resist him, but when his lips touched her own, she forgot the world and slipped into a space where there was nothing but herself and Andrew, and the touch of his body setting hers aglow.

For a fleeting moment, Nell wished he would take her, and make her his wife in deed, as well as in name. Then came a vision of Lady Fairley and the

102

puzzle of her presence at Chase, and a coolness entered her kisses.

Melford sighed inwardly as he judged her response. What had gotten into the chit now? he wondered lazily. Ah, well. It would keep. For now he meant to hold her and kiss her. The rest of the world could wait.

Chapter Seven

Nell looked out from the window to watch the party as they were leaving for the hunt. Eversleigh and Miss Wardmont were already in the saddle, while the other ladies stood about chatting as they waited for the remaining members of the party to appear. The horses were restive and Jane's horse reared, but she showed superb skill in the manner in which she brought him under control.

A noise in the room caught Nell's attention, and she turned to find Caroline Marlowe entering in a flurry of skirts. The scent of violets proclaimed her presence. "There you are, Nell. I have been looking for you everywhere. Since everyone is leaving, I thought we might have a comfortable coze this morning." Her ringlets fell artlessly over her shoulders.

Nell returned her smile and said, "Of course, Caroline. I have longed for a visit with you." Seating herself behind the tea table, she served Caroline before pouring a cup of the dark brew for herself and relaxed in her chair with a sigh. The steam curled up from her cup, and Nell watched it as she waited for the barrage of questions she knew was sure to come.

Before either of the ladies could speak, another interruption occurred. Melford strode into the room with his whip in his hand. Dressed in the hunt colors he looked magnificent, and her feelings were not successfully hidden as she smiled up at him.

He bent over her and said, "Excuse me, ladies. We're off." He dropped a quick kiss on her upturned lips, then said, "Enjoy your chatter, love, and have a large tea waiting for us when we return." He flicked a careless finger at her cheek and was off.

Nell heard him take the steps two at a time then his voice in the distance calling for his horse. She became aware of a certain quality in the silence that had invaded the room. When she looked at Caroline, she found her regarding Nell curiously.

Caroline took a tentative sip from her tea and smiled curiously. "I hope you don't think me impertinent, or vulgarly curious, Nell, but there is something enticingly odd about this marriage of yours."

At once Nell was all outraged dignity. "I don't believe I quite take your meaning, my dear."

"Don't fly up into the boughs, Nell. You used always to do so at the least provocation!" she said with a direct look at Nell that was amazingly disconcerting.

Nell couldn't keep the laugh from her lips. "Oh, Caroline, I am not up in the boughs, as you very well know. I truly didn't take your meaning."

"No, really, my dear. You have no need to pretend with me." Her dark curls bounced as she shook her head firmly. Realizing that only bluntness would serve, she continued, "You see, Nell, your marriage was so very sudden that all the ton is agog to know the reasons behind it. Then, when we arrived and found a young woman whose reputation is said to be slightly fast, a widow . . ." She let her voice trail off insinuatingly.

"It is not at all necessary for us to inform the ton of our movements, my dear Caroline. I hope you haven't joined the gossip-mongers?"

"Nell!" she gasped, hurt. "How can you say such a thing? We have been such friends, aside from our kinship. I meant no intrusion," she said in a mortified tone.

Immediately contrite, Nell said, "We are friends, Caroline, and I apologize for my words. I have not forgotten what a comfort you were to me when you came to visit every summer during our youth. With my father away so often, I always looked forward to your visits."

She considered for a moment, then said, "However, I can't bring myself to discuss my marriage with you. I *can* say that there were very good reasons for my marriage, and Lady Fairley is *not* my husband's mistress, as you seem to believe. I am distressed to be forced to make such a statement to you," she said violently.

"I never thought such a thing!" Caroline exclaimed untruthfully. "I am happy to hear you say so. How shocking it would be to be forced to entertain such a person."

"I am in full agreement with you, my dear Caroline. If I were you, I would look to my *own* laurels. I distinctly saw Sir Charles holding quite an intimate conversation with the lady in question for several moments last evening," Nell teased with a laughing glint in her eyes.

It was Lady Marlowe's turn to cloak herself in dignity. "How dare you say such a thing, Nell? What a low, vulgar thing to say! As if Charles would dare do such a thing!" she exclaimed in horror.

Nell laughed without restraint. "How does it feel, my lady?" she asked bluntly.

"I don't take your meaning," Lady Marlowe stated without circumlocution.

"The slipper is quite on the other foot, I see. I merely wondered how it felt," Nell enlightened her merrily.

When at last she realized that Nell was taking a jibe at her, Caroline joined her laughter without restraint. "Nell, you are a minx. You haven't changed a jot in the years we have been apart," she exclaimed, wiping the tears of laughter from her cheeks. "And I am truly sorry for prying," she added earnestly. "I can't seem to help it."

Having rid themselves of their curiosity, they enjoyed a comfortable coze for quite an hour. Nell had received in the morning post a letter from Fanny Brockheath informing her of her regret that it was impossible for her to be a member of Nell's house party. It seemed that Brockheath's grandmother had fallen ill and the family had been called to her side. Nell asked Caroline, "Do you remember Fanny Armstrong?"

Lady Marlowe said immediately, "How could I forget? The three of us were inseparable when we were children."

Nell said, "Well, I met her when I was in town. Did you know she had married Lord Brockheath?"

She nodded. "I remember. I was unable to attend the wedding, being *enceinte,* you know."

"She was going to join the house party, but was unable to come. I hope to see her again in the spring," she said with a sigh.

They enjoyed a comfortable visit, then Nell made her way down to the kitchens, where she assured herself everything was being prepared for the late luncheon the riders would be in need of when they returned.

The first of the guests were in the hall when Nell returned from the kitchens, and Lady Eversleigh cried out to Nell, "You should have come with us, my lady. We've had a jolly morning!" she added maliciously. Her eyes went to Melford, who had just come in behind Lady Fairley.

Lady Fairley's eyes met Nell's, and she flushed deeply upon hearing these words, knowing instantly the cause of Nell's consternation. She placed her nose in the air and said, "How true, my lady. The hunt was quite invigorating, I assure you. Of course, some of us were not around for the full course, but no matter." She shrugged her dainty shoulders and marched directly past Lady Eversleigh, who stared after her with daggers in her eyes.

Nell was beginning to wonder just who of the company was having an affair with whom, and a twinkle was in her eye as she found her hand taken into a light clasp. She looked at her husband and said, "I hope you had an enjoyable morning, my lord?"

"It is becoming much more so, I assure you,

milady. More and more by the minute." He nearly lost control of his features when Lady Eversleigh stalked away in the direction of the stairs.

As he dropped a light kiss on her fingers, Nell said, "Luncheon will be ready when everyone is down. I shall be waiting for you."

He ran toward the stairs, following the remaining members of the party, and soon disappeared in the direction of their room.

Nell chuckled as she entered the drawing room. It appeared that she wasn't the only one with suspicions, and for some reason that thought pleased her enormously. She frowned over her clasped fingers and considered Lady Fairley. For some reason that flush bothered her. It would take some consideration.

Chance gave her an opportunity to observe her quarry immediately. Lady Fairley was the first one down to luncheon, and she seemed pleased to see Nell waiting in the drawing room. "It appears I am ahead of schedule, my lady," she said uncertainly.

· Nell shook her head. "Not at all, my dear Lady Fairley. I am waiting for the remainder of our guests," she told her with a cordial smile.

The ladies watched each other warily for a moment, then Lady Fairley said diffidently, "I should like to apologize for my unladylike outburst earlier, Lady Melford. It was entirely unseemly, and I am sorry for it."

Nell smiled graciously and said, "Think no more of it, I beg you. Indeed, I was grateful to you, though in truth I have no business to say so. Don't give me away, I pray," she said with a laugh.

Encouraged, Lady Fairley joined in with her

laughter and added, "I can understand your feelings, my lady. Certain persons have been making pointed remarks all morning, and it is rather wearing," she said with a small frown.

Feeling more and more certain that her suspicions were correct, Nell warmed to her and said, "I know exactly how you feel, my lady. Some people habitually make odious remarks. I advise you to forget them all."

Soon their intimate conversation was interrupted as the other members of the party came into the drawing room. Sir Harry joined them on the sofa and soon a comfortable camaraderie developed between the ladies, and Nell could feel her affection growing for this young woman. Whatever she had been, Nell could see that she was not in the habit of enjoying private affairs with married men. Nell would have wagered her fortune on it.

Mrs. Wardmont had not felt able to join them for luncheon, so the numbers were equal, each of the ladies having an escort, with Nell and Sir Harry bringing up the rear of the small group.

Nell scolded him, although quite friendly, saying, "Sir Harry, you should be bringing in one of the other ladies. I don't expect you to devote yourself to me, I assure you."

He grinned down at her mockingly. "Don't deny me a small pleasure, my lady! I wanted to escort you. You have no objections, I trust?"

Nell shook her flaming hair and laughed, "None at all, my dear sir. I merely wondered how Melford is taking all this devotion."

From the look on his face, he wasn't taking to it at all. He was scowling in their direction while trying to listen attentively to Lady Eversleigh's never-ending spate of gossip. From the looks of things, she had decided to take a dig at Melford, who wasn't enjoying it in the least. Taking her arm firmly in his hand, he drew her quickly and firmly out the door.

All the talk at the luncheon table was of the hunt. Lord Eversleigh and Sir Charles discussed each stage of their morning until the final moment when both gentlemen had been in at the death. Each of the ladies added their bit, and soon the conversation was flowing smoothly.

Only Nell was uncomfortable. Her eyes met Melford's for a moment during the meal, and she was baffled by a certain measure of accusation she saw in them. She averted her face and the moment passed.

Hoping for a little privacy, Nell strolled out to the gazebo when the meal was finished and the party dispersed. It was hidden in a remote garden and was perfect for her purpose. The path was strewn with new-fallen leaves, and she enjoyed a quiet stroll, away from the bustling servants and the company of the guests. Nell sat for an idle moment on a bench in the gazebo and allowed her thoughts to roam at ease.

All was quiet, as everyone had felt the need for an afternoon of leisure after the excitement of the morning, and Nell was grateful for the respite from her duties.

Sir Charles and Caroline had retired immediately after luncheon, and Melford had gone off to the library. He was taking care of business, she assumed nonchalantly, wondering where the other members of the party had disappeared to.

The front of the gazebo opened on a view of the

small lake centered in the earl's property. It had been built years earlier by one of Melford's ancestors, and was a lovely spot, grown more beautiful with the passing of time. As Nell watched, she saw Melford come into view, and with a gasp realized that his companion was none other than Lady Fairley. She watched as they strolled along the quiet path to the lake, my lady's hand resting snugly within his arm.

Nell could hardly ignore her loveliness and wondered if Melford preferred her fairness to the flaming mass billowing about her own head. No longer caring to watch their intimacy, Nell turned her back on the scene, hoping to obliterate the sight from her memory, as well.

The sight of Melford with Lady Fairley was causing her anguish in another manner, and brought up some unpleasant recollections. Tormented by guilt as she had never been in the past, she remembered how she had forced him to continue with the marriage. Her heart smote her! She concluded that her pain was well deserved.

Never fainthearted, Nell refused to be daunted. If she was not his chosen lady, then she would do him honor by seeing to it that she did not disgrace him as a hostess. Her mind made up, she returned to the house, but inadvertently she came face to face with Melford and Lady Fairley as they returned from their tour of the lake.

His aloof smile chilled her to the bone, but she refused to let her feelings show. Smiling warmly, she said, "I hope you are enjoying yourself, Lady Fairley."

The lady's reply was equally as warm. "Oh, certainly, my lady. Lord Melford was just showing me

112

the lake. How lovely it is, to be sure." She glanced up at him innocently. "I am sure Lord Melford must be proud of it."

Nell was forced to grit her teeth but managed to keep a good face in spite of everything. She was fast coming to the conclusion that her feelings had been wrong.

Not giving Nell the opportunity to reply, Melford said, "I am certainly proud of it, my lady. I hope you are enjoying your visit." His brows rose inquiringly as he smiled at her warmly.

"I am certainly enjoying my stay at Melford Chase, my lord. You both have made me welcome." Their eyes met intimately.

"Then let us hope this won't be your last visit," he said gallantly.

"If you will excuse me," Nell said icily, "I was on the point of retiring to my chamber. I will meet you again at dinner." Her back was ramrod straight as she ascended the stairs and returned to her rooms.

She removed her gown, threw on a wrapper, and ran a brush through the unruly curls, wishing she could tame her volatile temper in the same manner. I might as well not have been with them, she fumed silently as she worked diligently at her curls. If he wants the chit, why must he flaunt her in my face? I warned him that I wouldn't stand for it . . .

On and on ran her thoughts. Round and round they went until she felt all awash with her feelings. Angrily she flopped on the uncomfortable sofa and stared out at the cloudy fall sky. A slight sound alerted her that she wasn't alone in the room, and she turned to find Melford standing inside the door. They looked at each other for several moments before he came into the room and sat down opposite her on one of the spindly French chairs.

He had discarded his coat and cravat and looked breathtakingly handsome as her eyes rested on his person for a moment before returning to survey the autumn sky.

Not taking his eyes from her rebellious posture, he asked negligently, "What is it, Nell? What has you up in the boughs this afternoon?"

Not being a fool, Nell had not the slightest intention of informing him of her thoughts and said with a sigh, "It is nothing. Nothing of importance." She shrugged her shoulders indifferently. It would be infinitely more humiliating for him to know how she hated the situation.

His gentle smile appeared in his eyes. "Come Nell. I am well enough acquainted with you to know when something has upset you. Tell me and I will take care of it."

She shook her head, refusing to answer, keeping her eyes on the open window. Her hair was spread out around her shoulders, hanging well below her waist. In her feminine emerald wrapper it gave her an allure she would have forcefully denied had it been made known to her.

Melford was entranced with her beauty. She seemed to him like a rich wine to be savored and enjoyed, not something to be used and thrown away as easily. He stretched his legs in front of him and made himself more comfortable, closing his eyes for a tired instant. Nell realized how hard he had been pushing himself to keep up with his duties as host and oversee all the neglected business of the estate.

She was instantly concerned. "You look tired," she said. "Have you had trouble with the estate?"

"A little " He roused himself to go on. "It is not the fault of the manager, but any estate needs the owner on hand. Things had gone nearly to rack and ruin and it has taken a lot of doing to bring them back to order."

Nell felt a pang of remorse at the thoughts she had been thinking about him. "Shall I ring for tea?" she suggested.

He shook his head. "I can think of nothing I would like better than my bed at this moment." He rose and pulled her to her feet. "Let us retire together, Nell." When she started to object, he put his hand over her mouth and said, "Don't say a word. Your virtue is safe for now, I simply don't have the energy."

He picked her up and dropped her on the bed before lying down beside her. It took a moment before his tense muscles relaxed, but soon he was fast asleep. It took longer for Nell to relax. She considered the events of the morning over and over, but soon she, too, was sleeping soundly.

A gentle knock aroused Nell, and thinking it was her maid come to dress her for dinner, she called out sleepily, "Come in," completely forgetting Melford lying so close beside her.

The door opened and Lady Fairley stepped into the room. Nell sat up in surprise and gasped as she realized that Melford was still in bed beside her.

Her embarrassment was nothing compared to that of her visitor. Lady Fairley blushed dreadfully and said, "I—I apologize for intruding, my lady. I didn't think . . . I mean . . ."

Nell attempted to regain her shattered dignity. She

115

pulled her wrapper about her tightly and said, "I'm sorry. I fear I was sleeping."

"I'll come back later," Lady Fairley said breathlessly, and fled.

Nell stared at the closed door for a moment, still hardly aware of what had happened, then lay back against the pillows. Nervously, she faced Melford. He seemed to be sleeping, and for once she hoped he was. He moved once in his sleep, then lay still. Nell lay back on the pillows and gave a sigh of relief, sinking deeply into the hazy mists of unconsciousness.

Chapter Eight

The days ran swiftly together, for Nell was kept busy. What with the hunting parties and planning menus, she was occupied for much of the time, which was unfortunate as several other matters had arisen to plague her, not the least of which was an uncomfortable interview with Lady Fairley.

Nell had been particularly embarrassed, harboring certain suspicions as she did; but taking her courage into her hands, she visited the lady in her room on the same evening of their contretemps.

Nell knocked on the door with a certain amount of trepidation. She hardly knew how to approach the lady, but was reassured when she came into the room. Nell was puzzled by the contrast in the lady's reputation and her behaviour, which did not appear at all forward or brazen. She scarcely knew *what* to think. Melford had shown her marked attention in town and again since she had been staying in the country, and Nell could not think what to make of the situation.

Lady Fairley flushed when she recognized her visitor, but showed no other sign of nervousness. "Come in, my lady. I was just finishing my preparations for dinner." She dismissed the maid and turned to Nell with determination. "I believe I owe you an apology, Lady Melford. I hardly know what to say." She looked so discommoded that Nell was immediately put at ease.

Nell shook her head. "That is not at all why I came, Lady Fairley. It is my feeling that I must beg *your* forgiveness for placing you in such a situation. I should have realized . . . It never occurred to me it would be anyone other than the maid." She blushed and added, "Of course under the circumstances I shouldn't have permitted even the maid to enter, but I was sleeping and automatically called out when I heard the knock on the door. I hope you will forgive me for embarrassing you so, my dear."

Lady Fairley rose from the dressing table and said, "It is not at all your fault, Lady Melford. I believe we can divide the honors. I hope you will convey my most sincere apologies to Lord Melford." She broke off with a blush.

Nell instantly felt a pang of jealousy. She was so beautiful, and Melford could hardly help being enamored of her, she was certain. She shook her head and added, "There is no need to inform his lordship of anything, ma'am. He is not aware of the matter. He was sleeping throughout the contretemps and I did not see fit to enlighten him. You may be easy in his company."

"Oh, thank goodness!" Lady Fairley exclaimed. "I

did not know how I was to face him, my lady," she added, though she looked at Nell in a puzzled manner, as if trying to straighten out her thoughts.

After a few more words, Nell excused herself and walked alone down the great staircase to the drawing rooms. Most of the guests were assembled, and to her consternation she found that she and Lady Fairley were the only remaining members of the party who hadn't come down. The entire group were to attend a dancing party being held at the home of a neighbor, Squire Treadway, and it was nearly time to leave.

Lady Fairley entered the room in a rustle of skirts, and there followed a short period of activity as the company donned greatcoats and cloaks and the carriages were called.

Nell found herself being bundled into their own carriage with Lady Fairley beside her. Melford and Sir Harry were seated across from them and they were off, the last carriage to leave. The Wardmonts were traveling alone, while the Marlowe's took the Eversleigh's in with them.

An uncomfortable silence prevailed while both ladies recalled the last meeting they had shared in Melford's presence, and both were suffused with blushes. Nell bit her lip to control the unseemly giggles that seemed determined to burst forth. When their eyes met, both ladies began giggling uncontrollably, unable to stop.

Melford surveyed them with a questioning glint in his eyes, while Harry exclaimed, "Well, well. Such high spirits. The ladies appear to have been up to mischief, Andrew." He rallied them for a moment before continuing his conversation with Melford.

The evening was a success, Nell was forced to

admit. Relieved of her duties as hostess for an evening, she was radiant with excitement. The Treadway family was cordial and excited about meeting the new earl and his bride. There were two daughters that had not yet been presented but were expecting the privilege during the next season. A son was down from Oxford for a visit (no one cared to mention that he was rusticating because of an episode with a dancing bear and the bagwig) and was in high spirits.

They sat down thirty to dinner, and Mrs. Treadway was flushed with the success of her party. The few neighbors who had been invited for the intimate dinner with the earl's party were flattered indeed to have received one of the coveted invitations.

Speculation was rife in the neighborhood. The earl had been absent from his home for so many years, although he had been well known in his youth, that everyone wanted to discover what manner of man he had become. There was also the matter of the new bride to be taken into consideration.

A few days before the Treadway dinner party a discussion took place between two ladies who had been asked to attend. The elderly dowager said quite openly, "I'll wager there is some scandal behind the marriage, my dear. It was so indecently sudden, you know."

Another lady ventured, "No, no, my dear Lavinia, they say they were promised since before the earl went away. It is all very romantic." She sighed gently, thinking of her own lost youth.

The dowager spoke again, "You are a fool, Lydia. You could always be taken in by a soft story."

Nevertheless, both ladies were present that evening, neither liking to receive their information

120

through the grapevine, having instead a preference for being on the spot, so to speak.

It was fortunate for the ladies in the party from Melford Chase that there were so many gentlemen in the party, for they were assured of partners for every dance. Any of the ladies would have scorned to admit of anxiety at having no acquaintance in the area, but the knowlege was of considerable relief, nonetheless.

When the musicians tuned up for the first set, the elder Treadway bowed gracefully before Nell, and she allowed him to lead her into the set with a warm smile. He was a pleasant companion, and Nell felt that her evening had begun auspiciously.

A quick glance showed Melford that the ladies from Melford Chase were all provided for, and he felt himself absolved from further duty and retired to the card room to enjoy a pleasant evening. Doing the pretty with every lady in the county was not at all in his line and he had no further intention than to do his duty.

Nell stood up for every dance, and enjoyed herself immensely, she told herself firmly. Was this not why she had forced Melford to acknowlege their marriage? she asked herself angrily, as she tried to ignore the void that had filled her heart as she watched Melford disappear in the direction of the card rooms, apparently having no intention of standing up with her at all.

Mentally shrugging her shoulders, dismissing the pain of Melford's lack of attention, Nell immediately plunged into a lively flirtation with Sir Harry, ignoring the scandalized looks from the various dowagers sitting on the sidelines.

Knowing from the outset that Nell was not sincerely trying to set up a flirtation with him, Harry joined in willingly, on the principle that it was much better for him to be involved than an innocent party who had been drawn unwittingly into it, led all unaware to the slaughter. His smile widened as he teased, "I don't believe I have had the opportunity of complimenting you on your looks this evening, my lady."

Nell preened and answered, "How sweet of you, Harry. Too kind."

He grinned at her and added, "I'm sure you were waiting breathlessly for my kind words, Nell." The movement of the dance separated them for a moment before they came back together.

A glint in her eyes warned him of the impending storm. "Be gallant enough at least to pretend that you believe me, Sir Harry," she hissed, although she held her head high.

"No need to fly into a pet, my dear," he replied with a grin that appeared to everyone in quite a loverlike guise. "I am well aware of your reasons for this start, but it won't work, you know."

Nell fluttered her eyes at him and smiled meltingly. "Really? Then perhaps you might explain yourself to me, my lord. I truly do not take your meaning." Her tone was designed to aggravate.

He shrugged in a barely perceptible gesture and led her to the side of the room to stand near Lady Marlowe and another gentleman, when the music ground to a halt.

The newcomer was talking animatedly with Caroline Marlowe, who made the introductions with a smile. "Nell, Sir Harry, such a delightful surprise, my dears. It seems impossible, but in this out-of-the-way place I have managed to find an old friend. Allow me to make known to you Viscount Lynman." She looked at her friend and said, "Gerard, my little cousin, Nell, Countess of Melford, and Sir Harry Claymore."

Harry was frowning fiercely, but Nell ignored his appearance and said with a laugh, "Sorry, Caroline. Lord Lynman and I made our acquaintance in London before we came home." She ignored Harry and gave her hand to Lynman defiantly. "How very good to meet you again in this out-of-the-way place, my lord."

Lynman bowed gracefully over her hand. "I could not long remain away from your beauty, my lady. I was forced to seek you out."

Nell blushed at these fulsome words. "You jest, my lord. I am well aware that you have many amusements in town."

He denied this forcefully. "The metropolis is a desert without your lovely presence, my lady. It was impossible to find amusement in your absence."

Nell colored up delightfully but was given no opportunity to reply to his flattering words, for Harry asked bluntly, "What really brings you to the neighborhood, Lynman? Are you placed nearby?"

Lord Lynman greeted Sir Harry cooly but with perfect propriety. "You wrong me, milord," he said. "You must know a man would travel far for the delights of a lady's company. I am staying with friends."

Lady Marlowe broke in on this to say, "Imagine, Nell. Lord Lynman has recently returned from the

East. He has been regaling us with tales of his adventures!"

Harry raised a cynical eyebrow but refused to comment. Nell said, "Of course, Caroline. It is very interesting." A thought occurred to her and she said to Lynman, "Viscount, why *have* you returned home so suddenly?"

He looked uncomfortable for a moment to Harry's delight. "Private reasons and all that, you know," he answered with a cold smile.

The lilting strains of a waltz could be heard as the musicians began playing their instruments, and the viscount smiled at Nell. "May I have this dance, my lady?"

Harry wanted to intercede but could not in all justice make a move. He had no right to interfere, and so watched with a frown as she placed her hand on the viscount's crooked arm and allowed him to lead her onto the floor. One would not have known from her appearance that she was wondering what Melford would have to say about Lynman's unwelcome appearance in the country.

When Harry recovered from his absorption, he turned to Lady Marlowe, who had remained standing at his side, and said courteously, "Will you dance with me, my lady?" She assented and they moved onto the floor to join the other dancers.

Harry looked down at her with speculation in his eyes. "I hope you are not up to anything, ma'am."

Lady Marlowe was all innocence. "What do you mean, sir? I assure you . . . !" she began huffily.

Harry studied her for a moment, then said, "If you are truly fond of Nell, then I fear you have done her a disservice by promoting her friendship with that gentleman, my lady," he said sternly.

For a moment her innocence left her. "And why not?" she asked. "Nell has every right to enjoy herself with her husband behaving in such a humiliating manner toward her."

In total surprise, Harry asked, "What are you talking about, ma'am?" He was becoming angry. "I assure you, Melford has not . . ."

Lady Marlowe's lip curled and she interrupted callously, "Don't speak to me of Melford, sir! Everyone is talking about his behavior with a certain woman we are both acquainted with. I am not the first to remark his constant attentions to Lady Fairley. Nell could hardly be in ignorance," she said angrily.

"But that is nothing. He is just being kind to the widow of an old friend. Melford would not so humiliate Nell," Harry defended hotly.

"Ha! Everyone has heard of his reputation. It is talked of regularly," she said angrily.

Their voices had grown increasingly loud as their discussion became more intense, and they were drawing the attention of some of the couples nearby. Sir Harry suddenly became aware of this and said in clipped tones, "I am surprised that a lady of your stature would admit to listening to common gossip."

For the remainder of the dance neither of them spoke, and he left her with a party of friends immediately as the music stopped. He went to the punch table, where he downed the innocuous liquid with unnecessary force and reached for another with a frown on his brow. Had he known of the conversation taking place on the dance floor, he would have been extremely upset. As it was, he decided it was time to go in search of Melford. Perhaps he would be able to deal with his wayward wife. Things were certainly worse than Harry had thought! Actually, it was Andrew's problem anyway! Why was he putting his troubles off on Harry? Sir Harry stalked toward the card room in search of his friend.

On the dance floor, Nell was being swung gracefully in tune with the lilting music, and enjoying it mightily. Lynman looked down at her and said with a romantic smile, "Beautiful, quite, quite beautiful. The weeks I have been away from you have been like years, my lady."

Nell grinned roguishly and replied, "Why, my lord, perhaps my ears deceive me. I am well aware of your reputation with the ladies. I daresay you never noticed my absence."

"I could never forget you, my lady. I trust I may be allowed to make up for my, shall we say, previous lapse?"

His blue eyes mesmerized her and she said, "I believe I must be persuaded that you have reason to continue my acquaintance, my lord."

"No, really, milady. You wrong me. What other reason could there be than to admire such beauty, even if it is from afar?" he asked boldly.

For a moment, Nell felt uncomfortable. The look in his eyes did not please her, but she continued the game of words and the moment passed.

Meanwhile, Harry had entered the card room and joined Melford at the table. He refused to take a hand, and as soon as he could he signified to him that he desired private conversation.

At the end of the next rubber, Melford withdrew

126

from the game and collected his winnings, then withdrew with Harry to a small terrace that joined the room.

Sir Harry leaned against a tall column built in the Roman style and turned to Melford with a serious expression. "I don't believe you were aware that a certain gentleman, Viscount Lynman to be exact, was to be present when you planned this outing?"

Melford had been staring into the gloom of the darkness, but he turned his head to stare at his friend when he heard this news. "No, is that fellow here?" he asked quietly.

"Certainly," Harry said tersely. "At this moment the fellow is on the dance floor with your wife," he added brutally.

"The devil he is!" Melford exclaimed. "What is he doing in the country?" he asked, giving Harry a sharp look.

Harry shrugged. "Who knows? The fellow is visiting friends, he says. It is my opinion he means you trouble. Beware."

Melford resumed his contemplation of the garden without speaking. He appeared to be giving some thought to the information Harry had given him, although he had taken the news more calmly than Harry had expected.

"What do you intend to do, Andrew? You can't let him involve Nell in any of his unsavory actions! And there's another thing." He paused for a moment indecisively. "I suppose you know what's being said about you and a certain lady."

Melford turned a quizzical gaze upon him and asked, "What of it? I care nothing for the gossip-mongers," he said carelessly.

Harry exploded. "Of all the care-for-nobodys! And I suppose you don't mind Nell hearing these rumors, either! It would surprise me not the least if that was what made her take up with Lynman in the first place!"

An arrested expression appeared on Melford's face, but he only said, "Here's a fine thing. You have been setting the grapevine alight with your behavior tonight! I am curious about this flirtation you seem intent upon having with the lady in question. And I thought you my friend!" he said with a glint of laughter in his eyes.

"Well, if that don't beat the Dutch!" Harry exclaimed angrily. "I spend the entire evening trying to keep *your* wife out of trouble, and you accuse me of trying to steal the chit from under your nose!" He turned back to the cardroom. "I am going where I shall be appreciated."

Melford grabbed his arm with a smothered laugh and said, "I am properly appreciative, Harry. But why?"

Harry stared at him incredulously. "If I have ever seen the devil in a lady's eyes, it was in Nell's tonight. And after the little talk I had with Caroline Marlowe, I am not surprised! I begin to believe you would be well served if Nell did run off with Lynman!"

"What are you talking about, Harry?" Melford asked, his brows drawn tightly together.

"It is plain as the nose on your face, Andrew. Nell and Caroline Marlowe are as thick as thieves, and if *she* believes you are having an affair with Charles Fairley's widow, then you can wager Nell thinks much the same thing!"

"But, Harry, you know perfectly well that I am

only being kind to the widow of an old friend," Melford exclaimed in exasperation.

"What I think is of little importance. It is what your wife thinks that is your most important problem."

He thought about the situation for a few moments, then said, "I need to mull this over for a while, Harry. I am returning to the ballroom. Do you join me?" he asked politely when he heard the music come to a halt.

Fortunately for his plans, Lynman happened to bring Nell to a stop quite near her husband, who was waiting patiently for her in the entrance to the ballroom. Of Harry there was no sign, he having providentially found a reason for keeping out of sight. It was none of his business, and he wanted no part of the coming scene.

Melford smiled unpleasantly when Lynman brought Nell to a standstill and said, "There you are, my dear. I have been looking for you. Are you ready to leave? I am certain you must be worn to the bone."

Nell stared at her husband in disbelief. He had not offered to stand up with her for even one set. She was of no mind to obey his every command at the moment. "Not really, my dear. Why, the evening has hardly begun," she exclaimed with an exquisite disregard for the facts. "I feel I could dance all night."

Lynman added fuel to the flame. "I would be happy to be your escort, my lady, if Lord Melford should desire to rush away from the delightful amusements we are enjoying."

Melford's eyes became flintlike and he said silkily, "I don't believe that will be at all necessary, my lord." He looked sternly at Nell, and for the first time she knew a certain fear in his presence. Holding out his arm he said, "My lady?"

Nell knew when she was beaten, though she was determined to go down fighting. Placing a hand on her husband's waiting arm, she smiled fleetingly at Lynman and said, "I enjoyed the dance, my lord. We have guests with us whom I am sure you will want to meet. Take tea with us tomorrow, do?"

Lynman smiled triumphantly at Melford and said firmly, "I shall be delighted to join you, my lady. Until tomorrow." He bowed elegantly and threaded his way through the throng of people toward his hostess to take his leave.

Nell was conscious of the tenseness of Melford's arm under her hand and wondered what he would have to say about her actions. She sniffed and put up her chin. She had no intention of allowing him to dictate to her. If he did not want her dancing with personable gentlemen, he should offer to stand up with her himself. So her thoughts raged on and on. Partially afraid of what her defiance might have caused, she spoke hardly at all on the return journey. Lady Fairley was forgotten in this new dilemma; all her thoughts were on the momentous episode that had brought the evening to an end.

Melford joined her in silence, and it was left to Harry and Lady Fairley to keep a semblance of normality in the rather tense situation. They discussed the ball at some length, praising the music, the guests, and the food. It seemed that the Treadways had outdone themselves on this occasion.

The other members of their party had remained at the ball to return at their leisure, and Nell was conscious of a feeling of relief. The two ladies retired immediately upon entering the hall.

Fearful that Melford might wish to speak with her about her behavior, she rushed upstairs with Lady Fairley, an anguished look in her eyes. When they parted, Nell said impulsively, "I would like to have a nice coze at your convenience, my lady. Would you object to joining me in my private sitting room on the morrow?"

Lady Fairley smiled an enchanting smile and said, "I should like nothing better, my lady." They parted with a brief hand clasp.

Nell entered her room with trepidation. She was fully aware that her behavior had been outrageous, in light of Melford's opinion of her association with Lynman, and she had no earthly idea what had come over her. Even the dreadful suspicions she had harbored concerning Melford and Lady Fairley was not enough to warrant acting directly against Andrew's wishes, and with one he hated so much!

Not wishing for any private conversation with his lordship, she rushed through her toilet, hoping to fall asleep immediately. It was not to be, for when Melford entered her room an hour later, she was quite wide awake, though she pretended to be asleep.

Downstairs, Melford had been discussing the situation with Harry, who after his initial intervention had no more desire to be drawn into what appeared to be developing into an explosive situation. Something would have to be done, and Melford was essentially a man of action. He would not allow his wife to be seduced by a known rake, one whom he had reasons of his own to distrust.

Andrew was quite puzzled by Nell's behavior with

131

Lynman. He could not believe that she was in love with him! Nell had returned his embraces so readily that he could not believe she would willingly turn to Lynman upon his reappearance. He would have to settle the matter once and for all. He sighed deeply before climbing the stairs to their room.

He entered the room quietly, though his temper had still not calmed completely. When he slid into the bed, Melford was immediately aware that Nell was not asleep. He was tempted to take her into his arms and show her that she was finally and irrevocably his, but the thought died before it was born. He would never take her without her willing consent, and in love. It was long into the night before either of them slept.

Chapter Nine

Nell was not refreshed when she woke the next morning. A pounding ache throbbed in her head, and she wished for nothing more than to remain where she was for the remainder of the day. Unable to enjoy the luxury of hiding from her guests, she wearily rang for her chocolate and, yawning widely, leaned against the pillows.

Melford, an early riser, was gone from the bed, and she was alone when she woke, though she well remembered his entrance into the room the night before. She was unable to understand his behavior, and at last gave up puzzling over it as her head was none too clear.

She was sipping her chocolate when he entered the room, and she nearly choked on the scalding liquid she was trying to swallow. Showing him a wan face she tried to smile, but it was too much effort.

He dropped to the side of the bed and picked up a slice of the buttered bread that she had not attempted to eat and took a bite, looking at her speculatively all the while. "You seem out of curl this morning, Nell. Could it be that society does *not* agree with you?" he asked with interest.

Nell glared at him and took another sip of chocolate. "I hardly think that is it. And I am perfectly well," she said defiantly.

He grinned at her and tugged a stray curl that had slipped from her nightcap. "No need to entertain me with Banbury tales, love. I have eyes in my head and am able to assimilate certain notions for myself."

"I am well aware of that," she said coldly. "Do you not join the hunt this morning? Or are the gentlemen laid up as well?" she asked cuttingly.

He laughed and said, "I'm off shortly. I wanted to speak with you privately, this morning," which brought a blush to her cheeks.

Nell's heart leapt into her throat. What did he want, she wondered frantically, trying to guess what he would have to say about her defiance of the night before. She stared at him with frightened eyes and swallowed convulsively, unable to forget his angry look as they had talked with the viscount on the previous evening. He had looked as if he was capable of any sort of violence.

Melford looked at her, letting no sign of his thoughts appear on his face. He wondered what her exact opinion of the viscount had been, and was still considering ways and means of settling the situation they had been landed in. He said suddenly, "If I remember correctly, my dear, your birthday is coming up shortly."

Nell stared at him, and relaxed. She smiled and

134

said, "Yes, in two days time. How did you know?" she asked curiously.

He smiled gently. "I made it my business to know, my love. Did you think I would not?"

Nell shook her head. "I don't believe I ever considered it, my lord," she said honestly, staring at her cup.

"Poor Nell," he teased with a glint in his dark eyes. "Hasn't anyone ever honored the day of your birth, love?"

"Of course. I often receive outstanding presents," she told him with a tinge of bitterness. "Once Papa thought to present me with a husband. A trifle late for the actual day, but better late than never, I believe is the old saying." She tried to smile, but failed.

He was startled by the bitterness in her voice, but didn't acknowlege it. "As your husband, I will remember the day in future," he said.

Nell petulantly turned her shoulder to him and said, "It makes no difference, my lord."

"In the sullens, my dear? And after *such a pleasant* evening. I'm shocked." He sounded not in the least shocked.

"It is not well done of you to tease me when I am not well, Andrew. What did you want to discuss with me?" she asked.

He sighed, his eyes softening, and relented. "Merely the notion I have conceived of a party to signify your birthday. Would you enjoy that?" He asked, a smile parting his well formed lips.

"It is not at all necessary for you to—to spoil me, my lord," she stammered as she sought for the right words. "I am well able to do without such an honor."

He took up her hand that had been clenched on

the coverlet and lifted it to his lips, which sent a tingle from the tips of her fingers to the pit of her stomach. "It is my pleasure, Nell," he said. "Do not deny it me."

Touched in spite of her firm resolve not to have anything more to do with him than necessary, she smiled softly and whispered, "An it please you, my lord, there is no more to say."

"Good, I am happy to see you so amenable this morning." He paused and looked at her for a long moment, before adding, "I have some things I must say to you. I do not like to mention it, and I can see you are ruffling up, but I must say this: be careful of forming friendships without due consideration of the consequences."

Nell flushed to the roots of her hair and picked at the coverlet with restless fingers. She was at a loss for words.

"I see you know the gentleman to whom I am referring. It would not do at all to be involved in an entanglement, my dear. I saw more than enough of him in town, and I would not think twice about putting a bullet through him were it to become necessary," he told her bluntly.

Immediately, Nell flushed again, this time in fury, and before she could contain the words said, "How dare you accuse me of such a thing, particularly in light of the circumstances," then bit her lip in confusion.

He was so still, she began to be afraid and it was a moment before he spoke. "I see you have been listening to the gossips, and all that muckraking. I hope you won't put me to the trouble of denying what you are so obviously thinking. You will remem-

136

ber that we are entertaining the widow of an old friend, nothing more." His eyes were steely, and Nell trembled in fear. Then he rose, after dropping a light kiss on her forehead, and picked up his whip. He headed for the door, where he turned back to look at her, all trace of his former sternness gone. "Oh, don't concern yourself with the preparations for the celebration. I shall attend to them myself." He grinned and added, "A surprise, you know," before closing the door smartly behind him.

A loud thump sounded on the door as he exited the room, and he grinned as he ran jauntily down the stairs. Everything would come about, he told himself happily.

Upstairs, Nell was furious. She grabbed the first convenient thing, which happened to be her hairbrush, and flung it with all her might at the door, where it landed with a resounding smack. She pushed the breakfast tray from her lap and jumped out of the bed to run to the window where the party could just be seen riding off down the lane. Angrily, she gripped the windowsill for a long moment, before finally turning her attention to her toilet for the day.

How dare he talk to her so, Nell raged. Was he telling the truth about Lady Fairley? Nell hardly knew what to think. Her thoughts were a jumble of confusion for a long moment. When she finally settled down, she was forced to admit that he had probably been telling the truth, bearing out what she had always felt about the lady. With a frown in her eyes, she wondered how she had come about her colorful reputation. Nell was still suspicious, but she was coming to believe that her first intuition had been right all the time.

Nell let her maid put her into a morning gown of her favorite lemon yellow. Her hair was dressed plainly, with only a few ringlets over one shoulder, then she went into her morning room positioned at the back of the house to pace the floor and ponder Melford's words. When Mrs. Thimble appeared as was her usual custom, Nell sent her away with a murmured excuse. She had forgotten her invitation to Lady Fairley and was surprised when a knock sounded.

Nell looked up from the window, and gasped. "Lady Fairley? What . . . ?" Recollecting her invitation, she summoned a weak smile and said, "Come in, my lady. Won't you sit down? Would you like some tea?" she asked in a nervous flutter.

Lady Fairley came into the room with her usual composure and took a chair close to Nell near the windows. "Thank you, Lady Melford. It is a lovely morning, is it not?"

Nell closed her eyes for a fleeting moment, and though she was hard put to it to find anything lovely in the day, she replied, "Quite, quite, lovely. I was just enjoying the beauty of the garden."

Taking the opportunity for movement afforded by ringing the bell rope, she mustered all her composure and put off her bad temper. Good breeding demanded she do no less.

The ladies chatted for the short time until the maid came with the teapot, and then Nell occupied herself with the business of pouring tea for her visitor, and then herself. When they were comfortably settled, Nell found herself asking the question that had plagued her since Melford had made his startling revelation. "Tell me, my lady, how it is you came by

138

your . . . colorful reputation? I find it difficult to understand."

Much to Nell's surprise and horror, the lady instantly lost all her composure, and her face crumpled piteously with big tears making their path down the smooth contours of her face. Her hands moved nervously, and she accidentally overturned the teacup she was balancing on her knee.

Uncomfortably aware of having caused this contretemps, Nell jumped up and cried, "Oh! I am sorry. I should have never . . . I don't know what made me say it . . . Let me help you clean this up." She was fully distressed as she saw Lady Fairley dabbing at her gown with a napkin.

Together the ladies mopped up the spilled tea and then seated themselves once more with fresh tea. Nell, ashamed of prying, said, "You may disregard my question, my lady. I had no right to ask such a thing of you. It was grossly impertinent, and I am vastly ashamed of my behaviour."

Lady Fairley wiped her eyes with a delicate lace handkerchief she had pulled from her sleeve and said, "It is quite all right, my lady. You see, I have often wondered the same thing myself, though in truth, I do know the answer."

Nell suddenly realized that there was much more to Lady Fairley than she had hitherto comprehended. She said, "If it will make you comfortable to confide in me, ma'am, I assure you the story will go no further."

Removing the final traces of her tears, Lady Fairley said, "I am happy to tell someone. I cannot talk with my family. They do not understand." She hesitated, then said, "Please call me Andrea. I hope we can be friends, my lady."

Nell smiled cautiously. She was not quite ready for intimacy but said, "Of course, and you must call me Nell." Her heart went out to the lady, who was obviously distressed, and she added spontaneously, "You must tell me all about it, Andrea, for I see that you are unhappy."

"Everything started with my marriage. Giles was older than myself, and we fell head over heels in love. He had been friends with Lord Melford in his younger days, but after his lordship left the country, Giles entered the army. He was still in the service when we were married. Not long after he had to return to his regiment and was killed in battle." She took a fortifying sip from her teacup and continued.

When he was killed, I was distraught, as you might imagine. I had one consolation. I was with child, and I savored the knowlege that I would have someone who would remind me of my dearest Giles. Then something happened, Nell. I just don't know what. The doctors never told me why, but somehow I began my pains early. My mother said it was the shock that caused it, but whatever the cause, my child was born three months early. He was too small to live. We buried him beside his father in the Fairley mausoleum." Her shoulders shook with the force of her emotion.

When she recovered herself Andrea went on. "Something happened to me after that. A wild and reckless feeling enveloped me, and I didn't want to control my actions. When my period of mourning ended, I went up to town, determined to leave the place where I had been so unhappy."

Nell nodded. "I can understand your feelings. I believe I should have felt the same under the circumstances."

Andrea smiled wryly. "There is more to come, Nell. When I reached town, I seemed bent on destroying myself with the ton. I flirted outrageously and committed every pardonable antic in my urge to remove the last vestiges of my grief. It did not work, and I soon learned the folly of such actions. Unfortunately, a reputation soon earned is not so soon lost. Everywhere I go, I hear the whispers but am unable to defend myself. But this I swear. I never had an affair with any gentleman, married or no. That I could not do." She paused for a moment, then added, "I must thank you and Lord Melford for all your kindness to me. I realize that I have no right to expect such consideration from either of you."

Nell felt ashamed of her former thoughts. After Melford's chastisement earlier that morning, she was positive that her suspicions were groundless and had done no honor to her own dignity or his, either. She stared at her clasped hands for a speechless moment, and when she looked up caught a glimmer of understanding in Lady Fairley's eyes. Before Nell could speak, that woman spoke again. "I can understand your feelings, Nell. I would have felt the same were I in your position. I trust no harm has been done through my presence," she said bluntly.

"Thank you very much. No harm has been done, I assure you. Perhaps this discussion will make a better understanding for us. I am sorry if I inadvertently caused you pain by my clumsy inquiries," Nell said contritely.

Lady Fairley accepted her apology graciously and

they went on to discuss more mundane matters. Soon she excused herself, and Nell turned with resignation to her neglected duties. She would have to placate Mrs. Thimble, who had grumbled at having her orderly routine disturbed. She went downstairs toward the kitchens, passing Miss Wardmont on the way.

Politely, Nell asked, "How are you this morning, Miss Wardmont? I trust you have recovered from our late evening?"

"Oh, yes. Nothing ever discommodes me, my lady. Mama is still abed this morning. Late evenings cause her infinite discomfort," she said with a confiding air.

"I am happy you are enjoying yourself. If you should happen to need anything at all, don't hesitate to ask for it. Now, if you will excuse me, I have an appointment with my housekeeper," she said with a smile.

"It must be quite a task running a house this size, milady."

"It is certainly one that requires attention." She went on her way to the kitchens.

Nell was busy for the remainder of the morning. Mrs. Thimble was in a grumpy mood, and it took a solid thirty minutes before they were able to get down to the work at hand. When she finished with the housekeeper, Nell went to the picture gallery in the west wing. She desired to view the portraits of Melford's family again. Mrs. Thimble had given her a hurried tour, but there was a particular portrait Nell had wished to see again. It was of Melford, painted only a few months before their marriage and subsequent parting. Nell wanted to study the portrait

142

in privacy, hoping to remember something of that other time.

What manner of youth had he been? she wondered. What had suddenly changed him enough to give him the drive to make his own fortune? Nell knew now that she had tumbled headlong in love with him from the beginning.

His portrait had captured the youth that was gone forever. With one hand on the back of a wing chair, and his head proudly high, his hair in the longer mode, he looked dashingly handsome. He had married her unthinkingly, then promptly forgotten her existence. She should be furious with him, but all she could remember was that he had been very kind to her in recent months, and she loved him. To be sure they had quarreled, but what couple did not? She reasoned. After his earlier words and her discussion with Lady Fairley, Nell felt she had been vastly troublesome to him.

When she came downstairs, the riding party had returned, tired but happy. Unfortunately, Nell was slightly late, and the party was seated at the luncheon table when Nell entered. Melford gave her an inscrutable glance before turning his attention to the lady on his left.

Nell groaned inwardly before apologizing. "Forgive me, all. I forgot the time." She slipped into her seat and allowed the footman to fill her plate with several choice delicacies.

On her right, Harry said, "What have you been up to, Nell? Andrew has been scowling since our return."

Nell said in surprise, "I don't know what you are

143

talking about, Harry. I haven't done anything. As I said, I forgot the time."

Harry chatted for a few moments with Lady Fairley before turning his attention once more to Nell. "You should have joined us this morning, Nell. I believe you would have enjoyed it fully."

Nell shook her head. "I never hunt, Harry. I don't like it."

He grinned. "It seems I neglected to tell you that we spent most of the time riding, not hunting. The damn-dashed, excuse me, fox was too wily for us." He shook his head curiously. "The animal got completely away."

Nell laughed happily. "I am in sympathy with the fox, Sir Harry." She grinned. "I feel it is better if I remain away. I cannot enjoy it."

"I know. Most females seem to be of the same opinion, although not all of them sit a horse as well as you do," he said with admiration.

Nell looked surprised and asked, "When have you seen me upon a horse? I don't recall riding with you."

"I chanced to come upon you in the park before your marriage, and after, for that matter too," he said ruminatively.

"I see," Nell answered. "Perhaps we can get up a riding party if the gentlemen aren't too worn down by their hunting exertions."

Suddenly realizing that they were neglecting their partners, they broke off their discussion, and the remainder of the meal passed pleasantly.

After lunch, the ladies gathered in the front drawing room to chat. The previous evening's entertainment was the chief topic under discussion. Lady

Eversleigh was saying, "Quite a delightful affair, I assure you, Mrs. Wardmont. In quite good taste. I shudder to describe the romps some of the London balls turn into."

Mrs. Wardmont asked, "Tell me, my lady, is it true that many of the faster ladies are willingly received into the ton?" She went on, "We have been out of the country for so long that we aren't perfectly conversant with the prevailing customs."

Lady Eversleigh laughed shrilly, drawing all eyes to her as she said, "My dear ma'am, you will be forced to accustom yourself to receiving all manner of persons. It is an acknowleged fact." She let her eyes stray to Andrea Fairley sitting with Caroline and Nell across the room.

Immediately, a bright flush covered Lady Fairley's cheeks as the implication of her words became plain to every person in the room. A tiny, uncomfortable pause ensued before Nell said, "I am certain things are not as dreadful as you say, my lady. Why, society would not allow it for a moment."

Lady Eversleigh smiled patronizingly, "Oh, you young things must learn for yourselves. I, for one, deplore the shocking state of society, my dear."

"It is true that many gentlemen are accepting more of the faster ladies," Caroline intercepted with a shrug. "I vow, it is nothing to concern one's self about. My solution is to ignore them all."

Giving the impression that her statement ended the discussion, she folded her hands in her lap and turned to Nell and Andrea with an impish smile. "La, Nell, what did you think of Viscount Lynman?" She rolled her eyes romantically. "He swept you into

145

the waltz so quickly, I had no chance to observe the two of you together."

In the background, Mrs. Wardmont was heard to mutter, "It seems to me that all the brazen females are not in London, my dear Lady Eversleigh."

When Caroline stared at her frigidly, she turned the comment into a cough. "Excuse me, so. I can't seem to rid myself of this pestilential cough." She rose and sailed from the room with her daughter in attendance.

When the door closed after her, Lady Eversleigh laughed again. "My, my, such ferocity, Lady Marlowe. Why, you frightened the poor lady to death, I vow."

"I don't relish being called brazen at any time, and certainly not to my face, my lady. It goes down rather badly, you know."

"Don't try to quarrel with me, my lady. I hadn't the slightest intention of referring to you, or your escapades when I mentioned the brazen ladies of society," she said with a pointed look at Andrea.

"Then, I suppose you were referring to me, my lady," Andrea said softly, clenching her fingers in her lap.

That abrasive laugh came again, and Lady Eversleigh said, "If the slipper fits, one must wear it, my dear." She laughed again uproariously.

Nell stared at her husband's cousin with loathing. Good manners or not, she intended to give this odious creature a set down! She opened her mouth to proceed when a diversion caused by the opening of the door stopped her mouth quite effectively.

Melford entered followed by Eversleigh, Marlowe, and Sir Harry. He halted for a moment when he saw the expressions evident on each female countenance. A quick glance at Nell informed him that something was amiss, but what he could not imagine.

Upon the entrance of the gentlemen, the ladies hurriedly composed their respective smiles into the usual society politesse, and appeared well disposed toward each other.

Soon callers were announced, and the uncomfortable situation passed. For Nell, it was quite a formidable task to force herself to be friendly with that odious woman, and she intended to inform Melford immediately. They had just cleared this hurdle when something occurred to upset the precarious balance of tension in the room. Nell had passed an innocuous remark to Andrea when Thimble opened the door and announced, "Viscount Lynman."

Nell's face was a study of confusion as she stared bravely into Melford's furious eyes. Her heart pounded as she waited for the scene that would surely come. She was sorry she had welcomed Lynman in so friendly a manner, and now sat with bated breath waiting for the results of her idiocy.

All eyes were upon the door when Lynman came in with his usual graceful stride, and Nell rose shakily to say, "Viscount Lynman, what a surprise!"

He bowed gracefully over her hand and seemingly unconscious of the other occupants of the parlor said, "Nothing could have kept me from your side. Each moment was like a year," he added charmingly.

He greeted Melford rather less effusively, saying, "Good afternoon, milord. I trust you are in your customary good health?"

Melford looked at him with a noticeable lack of

warmth and answered, "I believe I do as well as ever, Lynman. Are you acquainted with our guests?" he asked bluntly.

Lynman glanced around the room and with a spurious smile at Sir Harry said, "I believe Sir Harry and I have met before. In Venice, wasn't it?" He offered his hand in greeting.

Harry was hard put to it to reply in kind, but he managed to say, "I believe it was, my lord. I remember it very well."

Melford intervened, saying, "Then let me make you known to the remainder of the company." Beginning at the right of the room, he passed over Nell and said, "Lady Fairley, Lady Marlowe, I believe you are already acquainted with." He passed Harry, then said, "My cousin Eversleigh, Lord Marlowe, Lady Eversleigh." To the room at large he said, "Viscount Lynman."

Lynman smiled and bowed gracefully to each one in turn. When Melford finished his introductions he said, "Such charming flair, my lord. I must come to you for instruction, one day."

Melford unwillingly smiled and said, "It would be impossible to reveal my secrets in one day, my lord. It would take a lifetime."

Lynman silently acknowleged the hit before saying aloud, "Touché! I believe I know how I may take that."

Melford said firmly, "I am quite certain you do, Viscount."

Lynman shrugged off his seemingly innocent words and said, "If you will excuse me, my lord? Lady Melford seems to be trying to attract my attention." He walked across the room and seated himself gracefully at her side.

Sir Harry had been listening to the conversation with barely concealed impatience. "I would throw that cad out of my house, Andrew! You don't want him around getting up an affair with your wife!"

Lord Melford smiled gently and murmured, "Such heat! For what it is worth, my dear Harry, I have taken steps to prevent such a happening."

"Thank God for that!" Harry exclaimed under his breath as he watched the conversation taking place between Lady Melford and Lynman.

Conversation buzzed around the room, and in several breasts the question kept bounding about, *What was going on with Lady Melford and this known rake?*

Viscount Lynman planned to continue his flirtation with the wife of his old enemy, and this time he would get his revenge. He dismissed Nell as of little account. Her intelligence he counted negligible. If he considered it at all, he expected her to fall into his hands.

Unfortunately, things were not to fall out quite as he had planned. Although Nell had enjoyed his flattering attention, she had somehow fallen in love with her husband and hadn't the slightest intention of playing him false. Now that she was reassured as to his feelings for Andrea Fairley, she had no plans to make such a dangerously foolish mistake. Although Lynman tried to continue their earlier flirtation, he found Lady Nell curiously unreceptive.

Chapter Ten

The day of Nell's birthday party dawned bright and clear. Of the arrangements Nell knew very little, except that there seemed to be much activity going on when she wasn't present. Most of the ladies tended to stop their conversation when she approached, and several times various mysterious objects were whisked out of sight as she came into the room.

All this quite naturally whetted Nell's natural curiosity, and soon she was deliberately standing for a moment outside doors, trying to discover what was in the wind. Even Mrs. Wardmont was more urbane, and Nell felt a violent urge to discover the cause of such intense preparations!

Of Melford she had seen very little. Of Lynman she had seen more than enough. He had become a bit of a bore, but Nell hardly knew how to discourage his visits to the Chase after her earlier welcome. His posturing and extravagant compliments had become intolerable, but he seemed impervious to her detachment and continued to call frequently.

Although Melford disliked the viscount passionately, it was impossible to eliminate him from their circle of acquaintances in their close rural society. Although he was a known rake, he had always behaved more or less as a gentleman while in England and was still received in the ton.

So Lady Nell continued to receive the viscount, although she was careful to have someone with her at each of his visits, and always maintained a formal manner in his presence.

The birthday celebration was to mark the last night of the visit, for everyone had made preparations to journey to their homes on the morrow. Nell was more than happy to see the back of some of them. Mrs. Wardmont had been so disapproving that Nell had felt nearly an intruder in her own home, while Lady Eversleigh had made things nearly intolerable for everyone.

Being the wife of Melford's cousin, who also happened to be the current heir to Melford Chase in the event that Melford did not leave an heir of his own body, Lady Eversleigh felt safe in being as malicious as she pleased. And it pleased her to twit Melford frequently on his wife's newly acquired beau.

As a result, Melford, who was already steaming under the knowlege that he could not forbid Lynman hospitality in his house without causing a scandal, began snapping at anyone unwary enough to come within reach. Soon, everyone in the party was looking forward to the end of the visit.

Melford had asked Nell to remain in her suite on the morning of her birthday, and Nell spent a leisurely morning relaxing in bed with her morning chocolate and the latest gazettes. She studied the fashion pages closely to discover what the newest styles would be in the coming season, although she was still curious as to what Melford had planned for her tonight.

The ladies had also remained in their rooms during the day, making their preparations for the gala evening ahead. A formal dinner would be followed by a masked ball, to which Melford had invited most of the county, and quite reluctantly, Viscount Lynman was included in their number.

Although many of the genteel residents of the neighboring county felt that a masked ball was rather risqué, it was felt that with most of the dowagers in attendance it could not be anything but proper, and the young girls were in raptures at the prospect of going out in costume. Most had spent endless hours discussing their various ensembles.

Early in the afternoon, a footman entered Lady Nell's room with a large pile of boxes in his arms, which Lord Melford had sent up to her boudoir.

Surprised, Nell was about to investigate when the doors opened and Melford stepped into the room. His eyes were alight with anticipation as he lifted her fingers to his lips in greeting.

Nell smiled tremulously and asked, "What are these boxes, milord? I don't recall ordering anything from London."

He seated himself on the sofa and with a wave of his hand said, "See for yourself, my lady. The mystery will soon be solved."

Nell stared curiously at him for a long moment before obeying his casual command. Her fingers were a trifle unsteady as she dealt with the strings fastening the boxes, but soon she had the first one open. When she lifted the lid, she gasped at what met her eyes. A ball gown of the palest mint lay within, and when she removed it from the box, she found that it opened over an ivory satin underskirt that billowed around her in frothy ruffles. Though the decolletage was very revealing, the sleeves billowed over her arms to be caught in at the elbows with a ribbon before falling over her forearms in romantic ruffles.

As Nell appeared to be bereft of speech, Melford grinned and said, "Open the other boxes."

Nell reverently laid the gown on her bed and continued her search. The next boxes revealed undergarments in perfect coordination with the gown, and some dyed feathers to give it the final touch. When she had exclaimed over them all, Melford reached into his pocket and pulled out another slim velvet box, which he offered with a grin.

Unable to meet his eyes, she took the box knowing instinctively what lay inside. The emeralds twinkled up at her, and tears came unbidden to her eyes, which shone like the gems in her hands. She looked straightforwardly at Melford and said, "Melford, I hardly know—I mean, thank you." Her voice broke as she looked at him, and he rose to pull her tightly into his arms.

Nell placed her hands on each side of his face and said, "I don't know how to thank you, Melford. You should not have done all this."

His voice was gruff as he replied, "Don't be foolish, Nell. It is my pleasure and I don't want you to forget it."

Unable to control herself, she pulled his head

down to her and placed her soft lips against his. Instantly his arms tightened around her and she was pulled deeper into his embrace. When he released her, she laid her head against his shoulder and took a deep, trembling breath. His hand came up to caress her hair, which was falling down, giving her a vulnerable appearance. "Happy birthday, my dear. I hope to share many more of them with you," he whispered softly.

Nell flushed and burrowed her head further into his chest, hardly knowing how to reply. A hope that he might be foretelling the future took hold of her, but she refused to yield completely. He released her at her first movement away, and when they were seated again, she summoned a quivering smile before asking, "When am I to be allowed downstairs today? This room is becoming a trifle boring, my lord."

His brow lifted and he disconcerted her completely with a glance. "Oh?" His voice was smooth as he said firmly, "I wouldn't call it boring."

Her hands were clapped to red cheeks. "You are perfectly aware of my meaning, my lord," she exclaimed, furious at his implication.

He laughed and relented. "Actually, that is the other reason I have come. I ordered the groom to bring the horses round to the back door in twenty minutes. Can you be ready?"

Nell jumped up and said, "You go right down. If I am to change in that time I must hurry." She shooed him out the door ruthlessly. He laughed at her impetuousness.

Melford was waiting when she came down at the specified time. He commented approvingly. "Whatever I might find to fault you with, Nell, you are always on time."

Nell sniffed, but refused to give way to the urge to quarrel. The day was much too fine for bickering, and she was very pleased with him at the moment. It was the first outing she had been privileged to share with Melford since the arrival of the visitors. Melford threw her into the saddle and the mare sidled restlessly, but she quickly brought her under control by murmuring softly. Then Melford led the way out through the fields that edged the home lawns. Nell urged her mount to follow him, delighting in the feel of the wind on her face and hair.

They did not talk, neither feeling the need for polite conversation. Nell followed his lead, content to have him show her his home country in his familiar manner. Once away from the more inhabited countryside, they saw many of the forest animals scurrying about. Carefully avoiding rabbit holes, they passed almost unnoticed through the quiet woodlands.

When they came to a small glade, Melford dismounted and helped Nell out of her saddle. While he tied the horses to a tree, she picked up the skirt of her habit and strolled toward a soft, grassy knoll.

Melford caught up with her easily and together they seated themselves. Melford leaned back on his elbows to watch Nell, who was sitting nearby. They exchanged happy relaxed smiles, and Nell forgot to wonder about the reason for this unusual behavior.

He stared at the stream in the distance and said lazily, "Lovely, isn't it?"

Nell laughed uncertainly and answered, "Quite." She leaned her chin on her hand and said dreamily,

155

"There is nothing I love quite so much as the country in autumn. The colors are so beautiful."

"Ummhmmm," he murmured. "It was one thing I missed in my long years away from Britain. I used to dream of it, you know." He turned to stare up at her as she sat beside him. "I am very happy to be home."

"What was it like out there?" she asked curiously. "It seems so strange to travel so far from England." Then, a little strained, she added, "I have never been out of the country."

He stared into the distance. "You wouldn't have liked it. Hot and dusty. No rain. Totally different from Britain." He was silent for a long moment. "When this infernal war ends, perhaps we can travel. Things are so uncertain now."

"I would like that, I think," Nell said dreamily. "It must be very interesting to observe people very different from our own."

"It is," he replied slowly. "Their customs are so different, it is almost like stepping into another world." He glanced at her sharply, "In the Orient, I mean. Paris and Italy are not so very different. Not really. You would love Venice." He told her about the waterways that divided the city, and about the gondolas that made their way night and day.

Nell listened enthralled. His voice went on and on, drawing her from city to city as he described them to her, making her wish fervently for the opportunity to visit each one with him, to view the wonders for herself. The cool breeze moved around them, lulling them into a gentle mood, causing them to forget for a short time the differences that had sprung up between them.

Gentle magic was in the air. Nell felt it pulling her toward her husband and wondered briefly if he, too, felt the stirring of romance that was about them. It seemed that he had, for he wasn't at all anxious to return home to the duties that waited for each of them.

But every idyll must end, and so it was for Nell and Lord Andrew. With a sigh he noticed the lowering sun in the western sky, and jumped to his feet agilely. Offering his hand to Nell, he drew her more slowly to stand near him. "We must be getting back." He smiled down at her, his dark eyes glowing with happiness and mischief. "Your day is really just beginning, my love." Nell looked up at him for a moment, then said, "I am sure I do not know what you have planned, my lord. Everyone is so secretive about it."

He helped her to mount with a smile. "And so am I, my dear. I have no intention of giving the game away at this stage. You will know soon enough." He mounted easily and they made their way homeward in a slow, easy manner.

When they reached the house, he said, "I want you to go up to our room and rest until dinner. You are not to venture from the room until I come for you. Promise?"

Nell smiled dreamily and murmured, "Promise." She floated on a blissful cloud up the stairs and settled down in her room to dream of a pair of dark eyes under an untidy mass of black curls that stared at her so disarmingly.

Her maid woke her an hour later, and urged her to dress as the time had somehow sped. Nell eagerly began her preparations for the evening. She was curious as to her lord's plans for the evening, and wanted to miss none of it. The girl pulled Nell's hair into a high cascade of ringlets that obligingly fell over one shoulder, leaving the other tantalizingly bare. A satin ribbon of the palest green was threaded through the curls, and when she placed the emeralds round her throat, she could only stare for a long breathless moment.

With an expert eye, Melford had instinctively chosen the colors that would bring out the hue of her eyes and the flaming brightness of her hair. An ivory satin wrap was draped over her elbows, and she was ready to go down. As if he could see through the doors, Melford stood inside his dressing room and knocked politely before letting himself into the room. Nell turned from the mirror to greet him, and was shocked into speechlessness. He was wearing ivory satin smallclothes, and his evening coat was of the emerald of her gems. His tiepin matched her jewels, and also the pins of his cuffs. In all, Nell was well pleased and managed a weak smile.

He said easily, "Nell, my dear, you are positively ravishing. You are always lovely when you are properly gowned." He hesitated, then laughed a little. "That did not come out quite as I intended."

Nell stared at him inquiringly, apparently unable to utter a word for herself, and he tried again. "You're as beautiful as always, Nell." At last she was able to speak and she said, "I might say the same of you, my lord. I have never seen you in such looks."

His eyes twinkled and he asked, "Would you say beautiful? I find I dislike the implication."

Nell joined in his laughter, and after a moment

said, "You are very jolly tonight, my lord. What could possibly be the reason?"

"Nothing in particular." He shrugged his broad shoulders elegantly.

Nell went for a final look in the glass before asking, "Do you mean to inform me what I may expect to find when I descend?" she asked curiously.

He shook his head. "I mean to extract the full measure of my surprise, ma'am. I hope you enjoy it."

"I am not enjoying it, sir!" she asserted stoutly. "If I don't find out soon, I shall go mad."

He laughed and said, "You haven't much longer now. Shall we descend?" He offered his arm, and Nell placed her hand on it willingly.

When they came to the top of the staircase in the main hall, Nell blinked her eyes at the blaze of lights. Candles lit every nook and cranny of the grand hallway. The public rooms were open, and light glowed from the open doors.

Nell entered the drawing room on Melford's arm and was immediately grateful for the support of his arm. The room was filled to overflowing, and it was obvious from the sight of the elegant attire and jewels that their guests considered this night a special occasion. The crowd hushed for a moment while everyone took in the flawless appearance of the earl and his lady. Then Miss Wardmont rushed over, looking lovely in her debutante white, and exclaimed, "Isn't it exciting, my lady? A ball! I can hardly believe I am being allowed to attend!"

Nell smiled at her eagerness and said. "Lovely, isn't it. I must confess to being a mite excited myself."

Before they could continue, Lady Marlowe interrupted. "La, Nell, you look lovely tonight. I vow, that gown is ravishing!"

For a brief moment Nell's eyes met those of her husband. Then she said, "Why, thank you, Caroline. A birthday gift, of course."

Lady Marlowe inspected Nell's toilet carefully before saying, "Jewels, too. Emeralds, no less."

Nell nodded again, not in the least put out by her forwardness. She had long since become inured to her curiosity. "I don't suppose you could tell me what is going forward tonight, Caroline?" she asked.

Melford excused himself and went across to join the men. Lady Marlowe answered with a tinkling laugh, "Hardly, Nell. Melford would have my head on a platter. You will have to enjoy each moment of the evening as it comes."

Andrea Fairley joined in the conversation. "Lord Melford swore each of us to secrecy, Nell. It has been such fun. I have a small gift for you." She placed a small box in her hand.

Nell opened it and gasped. "Andrea, this was not necessary!" On a bed of white satin lay a small pearl brooch. Nell held it up for all to see. Each member of the party had something for her, and Nell was tremendously surprised when Mrs. Wardmont handed her a small package. It was a small silken reticule, and quite beautiful. Her gifts varied from a lovely painted ivory fan from Harry, to a beautiful gilt box in which to hold her jewelry, from Lady Eversleigh. Nell thanked each one prettily before ringing for her maid to bear the gifts safely to her suite.

Dinner was to be an intimate affair, with only the members of the house party present. When Thimble announced the meal, Melford immediately offered

160

his arm to Nell, saying quietly, "As you are the guest of honor, it is only fitting that you should be taken in on the arm of the host, my lady." His dark eyes searched her face as he spoke, and his arm pressed hers tightly against him as they entered the dining parlor.

Dinner was a merry meal, and conversation flowed without interruption. Although she took part in the conversation with each of her dinner partners, Nell was constantly aware of her husband's eyes on her from the head of the table.

The gentlemen had just joined the ladies in the parlor after the meal when the first carriages were heard on the carriage drive, and Nell allowed Melford to lead her to their place at the head of the stairs. He murmured amusing anecdotes to her between introductions, causing her to giggle at all the wrong times. The first guest was masked, and Nell realized with a thrill that the ball was to be a masquerade. At the first opportunity she whispered, "A masked ball, how lovely! Thank you!" before turning back to the business of greeting their guests.

Viscount Lynman made his appearance and caused a moment of awkwardness for Nell, who felt Andrew stiffen as he came up the stairs. She was at first surprised to find that Melford had issued him an invitation, but then realized that however much he might dislike the man he would never air his difficulties in public and would act as a perfect gentleman at all times.

Lynman smiled down into Nell's eyes. "Good evening, my lady. Ravishing, as ever," he said outrageously.

Nell acknowleged his compliment with a cold

161

bow, and replied, "Why, thank you my lord. We are happy you could honor us with your presence."

"The pleasure is all mine," he said instantly. "I hope you will save a dance for me, my lady. Such a privilege to be allowed the honor of your hand."

She laughed before turning to the next arrival and said, "Perhaps it can be arranged, my lord."

When the last guest had entered the ballroom, Melford turned to her with a smile and presented her with a strip of satin he had procured for her mask. He tied it slowly before offering his arm for the opening set. The evening had begun.

From the moment Melford took his lady into his arms, Nell seemed to float in a dazzling haze somewhere up near the ceiling among the brightly polished chandeliers. The younger set had thought of many outstanding costumes, and Nell was highly amused by their antics. A pirate danced by with a goddess on his arm, and Nell was certain she saw an old seaman in the company. It was a fantastic evening.

After one set, Nell was standing near Lady Fairley, who had been dancing with Sir Harry. They were deep in conversation and hardly noticed as she approached. Nell's eyes narrowed in speculation as she considered the match. Then she shook her head. Harry had no intention of settling down to the quiet of married life, that was certain.

Nell was conscious of interrupting their tête-à-tête. "Are you enjoying yourselves?" she asked.

They both jumped in surprise, then composed themselves admirably. "Lovely party, Nell." Harry answered. "Quite a squeeze for the country."

Nell grinned. "Trust Melford to do things spectacularly."

Andrea smiled mischievously and said, "You haven't seen anything yet, Nell. The evening is just beginning."

Nell gave her a puzzled glance but refrained from replying when Viscount Lynman came up to claim his dance. Nell watched him a trifle apprehensively but went with him willingly enough. She hoped he wouldn't make a spectacle of her tonight.

It happened that their dance was a waltz, and Nell felt distinctly uncomfortable when his arm slid about her waist. He stared down into her face with a smile and said, "I have waited all evening for this opportunity, my lady."

Nell risked a glance and asked, "Really? I can't imagine why."

He laughed coarsely and said, "I should have thought you knew the answer to that perfectly well, Lady Nell."

She stiffened immediately and told him, "I have not given you permission to make free with my name. You may call me Lady Melford."

Lynman stared about them for a moment. Then, before she knew what he was about, he danced her out the open windows to the terrace. They came to a stop several steps from the brightly lit doors, and Nell began to struggle in his embrace. He laughed and said, "Come now, my lady. You are not so averse to my advances."

Nell gasped in outrage, but was unable to remove his arms from her waist. She opened her mouth to scream when a voice from behind her said, "How

163

naughty of you, Nell. I thought I was the only gentleman you were trysting with this evening."

Nell stared thankfully into Lord Marlowe's kind face and said, "Why, Charles, I was waiting for you when Lord Lynman joined me for some conversation. I hope I haven't kept you waiting?" She managed to steady her voice, although her face was still flushed.

He shook his head and replied, "Not at all, my dear." With a glint in his eye he said to Lynman, "I thank you for keeping her ladyship company until I could release myself from my other obligations, Lynman. I pray you will now excuse us?" His voice was nonchalantly polite, but there was no mistaking the firmness of his intentions, and Lynman could do nothing without making a scene.

He bowed gracefully and said, "Thank you for the pleasure of the dance, my lady. If you will excuse me?"

Nell and Sir Charles watched without speaking as he left them alone in the semidarkness of the terrace. Sir Charles said, "I thought he was molesting you, my lady. I hope I didn't intrude."

Nell dabbed at a wayward tear with her handkerchief before saying shakily, "I had no idea he would do such a thing. We were dancing one moment, and the next he was pushing me through the open doors. I was not able to stop him."

Sir Charles patted her hand gently. "Don't let it upset you, my dear. Now, come, we must rejoin the party." With the most graceful of movements he maneuvered her back into the ballroom and into the waltz that was still in progress. Nell could not be certain, but she suspected that Sir Charles must have informed Melford of their contretemps with Lynman, for the earl remained attentively at her side for the remainder of the evening.

During supper they sat quietly alone at a small private table for two that Melford had set up in a secluded corner of the room, and he laughed and teased her constantly. His eyes dwelt on her white shoulders where the mass of curls fell away in their usual disheveled manner. "Are you enjoying your birthday, Nell?" he asked quietly as his eyes feasted on her loveliness.

Her sparkling eyes told the tale, but she answered, "Andrew, it is wonderful. I have never been so happy in my life."

He returned her smile before leaning back to take a sip of the punch the waiter had placed before him a moment earlier. He said casually, "The unmasking will take place after the fireworks are over," and enjoyed her gasp of pleasure.

"Fireworks," she breathed. "Melford, I have always wanted to see the display at Vauxhall, but there was never an opportunity."

Melford lifted her fingers to his lips with a gentle smile and said, "I thought you would like it, my dear. Enjoy yourself."

All eyes were upon them, the dowagers looking on in pleasure at the devotion so openly displayed between the earl and his bride. Viscount Lynman watched their actions broodingly, and Nell shivered when her eyes chanced to meet his. It was with considerable relief that she received his excuses before he made his way home.

Melford claimed Nell's hand for the supper dance, and they were the first couple on the floor. They looked oblivious of the other guests, and no one was truly jealous of their happiness.

When it came time for the fireworks, Melford escorted Nell to the gardens, which had been lit with lanterns placed intermittently along the path to the display. The younger members of the party rushed out to gain a good position for viewing the proceedings. Many of the mothers looked about for wayward daughters, who seemed to have lost all sense of propriety in the anonymity of the masquerade.

The guests applauded repeatedly as the sky was lit over and over again by the brilliant showering designs. When everything was over, the unmasking began, and soon the party broke up.

Nell and Melford stood at the doorway accepting thanks for a congenial party. Many exclaimed enthusiastically over the entertainment, and Nell was thrilled with the ball's success. When the last guest had gone, Nell turned a tired smile to Melford and went up to her room with the other ladies of the house party who were retiring for the evening.

Everyone was in good spirits after the ball and chattered good-naturedly until they were separated at the head of the stairs. Although still imbued with the high spirits caused by the celebration, some had turned their thoughts toward the long journey they must begin on the morrow.

Nell went into her chamber and leaned tiredly against the door for a long moment before making an effort to prepare for bed. She stared at herself in the glass, hardly recognizing the radiant creature that smiled back. Finally, she hugged herself sensuously and began her nightly ritual. She reverently removed her jewels and locked them into a drawer of the dressing table. She firmly intended giving them to Melford in the morning to be placed into his safe.

When she was dressed in a sheer minty nightdress, Nell threw on a wrapper and went to stare into the courtyard. The sky was black as it was still several hours until dawn. Leaning her elbows on the window sill, Nell thought dreamily about the party, and about the way Melford had remained close to her the entire evening.

Nell never noticed the opening of the door, or the entrance of Melford, who had donned his dressing gown. He stood near the bed watching her as she dreamed by the windows, a smile flickering across his face. Moving quietly, he snuffed out all the candles in the room except the one by the bed.

Noticing the sudden darkness of the room, Nell looked up, and there he was. She smiled gently, welcomingly, and without words he pulled her into his arms. His lips touched hers and a flame started within her, kindled by his touch. She slid her arms around him, forgetting everything but the love she bore this strong yet gentle man.

Andrew murmured her name softly. "Nell, my sweet Nell. I must have you. Do you not know what I feel for you?"

Nell stared into the serious eyes that gleamed above her, and her heart was touched. She swallowed a gulp and said, "I believe I do, Andrew."

He asked softly, "Do you love me, dearest?"

Nell stared at him for a long moment. Her heart pounded as she gave herself irrevocably into his keeping. "Yes, I do. I love you, Andrew."

An uncontrollable shiver shook her, and he said

167

solicitously, "You are cold." He turned her about and said, "Get into bed."

He closed the window while she slipped off her wrapper, and got into the bed, pulling the covers up to her chin. Nell watched as he crossed the room and removed his dressing gown, and she thought whimsically that it wasn't at all as she had imagined the prelude to becoming a wife might be. When he got into bed, she giggled. "What do you find so amusing, my lady?" he asked as he drew her tightly into his arms. His lips searched out the softness of her neck, and moved lower.

"It is just that it is not happening as I thought it might, my lord," she said with a blush.

He cocked a brow and asked, "What did you expect?"

"I don't really know."

"Then perhaps we can postpone this conversation," he suggested before claiming her lips in an ardent kiss.

Nell followed his lead breathlessly as he initiated her into her marital duties, and when he became a part of her she hardly noticed the minute accompanying pain, so deeply had he engaged her feelings. When he moved away, she felt a strong sense of loss, only to be instantly relieved when he pulled her back into his warm embrace.

Nell snuggled closer, and lightly moved her fingers across his hard, bare chest, causing him to chuckle. She looked inquiringly at him and he said, "If you want to sleep the remainder of the night, you won't do that, my little love."

She slipped her arms around his firm neck and said audaciously, "Why not? I like it."

His chuckle was infectious and she could feel his chest heaving under her fingers before he said, "Who could resist such a delightful invitation?"

Nell began to exclaim, "But it was no such thing!" when his mouth stopped her words completely. The remainder of the night was spent in precious moments discovering the delights of love. Andrew loved her gently, with respect, then roughly with passion. They fell asleep as the sun rose slowly in the east, Andrew's dark head nestled on Nell's breast and her arms clasped tightly around him.

Nell awoke to find Andrew tugging her auburn curls. When she opened her eyes, he said, "I love you, Nell."

Her arms automatically encircled his head and she whispered, "I love you, too, Andrew." Their lips met in a warmly passionate kiss that set off another shower of stars in her head that rivalled the fireworks of the night before.

Melford remained with her for an hour, whispering delightful nonsense into her receptive ears. When he left her to dress, she gave a happy laugh full of love and joy.

Chapter Eleven

For the rest of her life, Nell would remember the next few weeks as the happiest she had ever known. Although they had never taken an official wedding journey, the sweetness and consideration Melford showed her was worth more to her than all the wedding trips in the world. Andrew was a gentle, considerate lover, slowly teaching her the ways of the marriage bed, and Nell fell more deeply in love with him every moment they were together.

The morning after the ball, she rose languorously to see her guests off on their journey home. Although Nell was genuinely sorry to have Andrea and Caroline leave her, she comforted herself with the thought that they would all meet in London during the spring season. With promises to write and quick hugs, they were off.

Andrew and Nell had watched the last of the carriages roll away before returning indoors. A gentle flush covered Nell's cheeks as she and Melford met alone for the first time since they had been together in their room that morning.

He casually threw his arm around her shoulders and led her into the library where, due to the coolness of the day, a small fire had been lit. "Come in and get warm," he invited. "I will pour us a glass of wine and then we can be comfortable."

Nell seated herself in a wing chair near the fireplace, and watched with tender eyes while he filled two glasses with wine and placed them on the wine table near his chair. When he seated himself without bringing her the wine, she looked at him with a question in her eyes.

He laughed and opened his arms to her. "Come here, my lady. I want to talk with you."

Mischievously, Nell said, "I am quite comfortable, my lord. Surely we can converse from this distance?"

He shook his head and said nonsensically, "My lady, I require private conversation with you."

Nell laughed and relented, for truth to tell, she had no desire to resist him. She rose and sat gingerly on his knee, but he pulled her tightly into his embrace. "I have wanted to do this all day," he whispered roughly into her ear. "Thank God we have the house to ourselves again!" he added fervently.

Nell laughed and offered him her lips. He was quick to take advantage of the opportunity and thus there was little conversation for some time. When at length he released her, Nell sat up a little straighter and sipped the wine he offered. Her cheeks were rosy, but she gallantly tried to restore a semblance of normalcy to the occasion. "It is pleasant to have the house to ourselves again. I enjoyed having guests, but it is always nice when the house is quiet again."

He let his desire for her show in his romantic dark eyes, and she blushed at her thoughts. He pretended not to notice, and said, "Just so," as he sipped from his glass.

Nell babbled on. "I will miss dearest Andrea and Caroline, but we will be able to visit during the season." Her heart was pounding and she could feel the strength in the arms holding her so closely.

He said very gently, "Although I like Lady Fairley very well, and also Lady Marlowe, I have very little interest in discussing either of them at the moment, my dear." His eyes rested on her mouth, and for a moment Nell felt as if he were kissing her. He removed the glass from her hand and said, "I love you, Nell, and all you can think about are our departed guests. For shame."

She turned to him and fully yielded to his embrace. Her arms slid around his shoulders and she pressed her lips impulsively to his. She murmured against his mouth, "I love you, I love you, I love you."

The hard pressure of his lips stopped her words, but not before she heard him whisper in return, "I adore you, my darling." His hands moved searchingly over her yielding body and his fingers deftly unbuttoned the tiny buttons down the front of her dress as he searched for tender flesh to caress. Nell shivered as his hands wandered aimlessly over her body and a tenseness invaded her being. Once again she experienced desire, true and undisguised desire for the man holding her so gently in his arms. She whispered, "I adore you, Andrew." Her breath came swiftly and she said, "I need you, my dearest."

In a moment, she found herself on her feet. Surprised, she opened her mouth to find out what he

172

meant by it, when he rose and placed a hand over her mouth, halting her words. He swiftly buttoned her gown and took her hand in an iron grip before saying, "This conversation can more profitably be continued upstairs."

Before she knew what he was about, he had picked her up and carried her up the stairway to their suite. She closed the door as he carried her through, placed her gently on the canopied bed, and leaned over her, whispering, "Now, we can be comfortable, darling."

What followed was a sensuous seduction, the likes of which Nell had never imagined. He made love to her slowly, bringing her desire to a fever pitch. He removed her garments one by one. He was in no hurry today. When finally he took her, she gave herself to him completely.

When it was over, they lay quietly together, murmuring lazy endearments into each other's ears. Andrew said, "I have longed for you, my love, for such a time."

Nell questioned, "Truly? I didn't know."

"Yes," his voice came huskily. "It seems forever."

They loved the afternoon away in the great canopied bed. When it came time for dinner, Mrs. Thimble served it on a tray in their room, where they could continue to be alone in their private world.

Andrew teased Nell, enjoying the bright flush that covered her cheeks so suddenly. They talked about the previous day, and the ball, and Nell told him seriously, "I have never enjoyed a birthday more."

"I am glad I was able to please you, love. It was rather amusing, don't you think?" He grinned at her as they remembered several comical incidents that had taken place toward the end of the evening. During the latter half of the ball, Mrs. Treadway had been seen coming huffily from the library in a definite hurry. Mr. Rickenbauer, a retiring, very timid gentleman, had been seen to leave shortly thereafter, and it was obvious to everyone that a feeling of courage engendered by the overabundant consumption of Lord Melford's punch had caused him to behave improperly. A large red handprint on his cheek gave mute evidence to this when he had made his excuses to the Melford's a short time later.

And so the day had passed, first in their loving one another, then teasing. Nell fell in love with him all over again. As for Melford, her smile warmed his heart, and he was glad he had persuaded her to marry him, forgetting that it had been she who had insisted on maintaining the marriage against his wishes.

Day followed day, and Nell was more in love with her husband than ever. Soon a routine was established, and she resumed command of the big house with something of her usual competence. Andrew's work kept him busy, and some days he was forced to travel all day from one farm to another to see that things were in order.

Several days after the birthday ball, Andrew rode out early in the morning and was gone all day. Late in the afternoon the door knocker sounded. Alone in the parlor, Nell was having her usual afternoon tea and welcomed the company, having heard the arriving of the carriage. Hearing footsteps in the hall, she smiled welcomingly at the door, only to have her smile freeze on her face as Thimble announced, "Viscount Lynman."

Gathering her wits about her, Nell rose from be-

174

hind the tea table and asked with a forced smile, "What brings you in this direction, my lord?"

"Can you possibly wonder, my lady? But your lovely self, of course," he assured her fulsomely. "You must be aware that I have become your slave for life."

Nell removed her hand from his and answered, "I wasn't aware of it. Won't you sit down?" She seated herself safely behind the tea tray and poured him a cup. "Share a cup of tea with me, my lord. I'm certain it will cool your ardor."

He looked outraged and changed his tactics. With narrowed eyes he surveyed Nell and wondered what had happened to the chit. She was different since their first meeting after his arrival in the country. Shrugging mentally, he thought if Melford was in love with the chit, it would make his revenge more enjoyable.

He accepted the tea complacently and inquired, "Where is Lord Melford, my lady? I did not see him as I came in."

Nell replied calmly. She noticed his narrowed eyes and a shiver went through her. He was beginning to frighten her. "My lord has ridden out to the farms," she said lightly. Nell was suddenly curious. This man certainly had no liking for Melford, and his protestations of love for her rang blatantly insincere. She decided to pry a little herself. "I believe you knew my husband in Venice, Viscount? Is that correct?" she asked with a pleasant smile.

His eyes widened at this direct attack, and he answered smoothly, "Yes, we were well acquainted in Venice and in England before that."

"I wasn't aware that your acquaintance went back

175

so many years," Nell said. "Were you friends in those days?"

His curiosity was now truly piqued. "What makes you ask, Lady Melford? Are you concerned about my association with your husband?"

"Whatever can you mean, sir?" Nell asked, all innocence. "I have seen no cause for concern."

He set his teacup on the table almost roughly. "It seems very odd, this sudden interest in your husband's past experiences."

Unable to contain herself, she retorted, "And it seems very odd, your sudden interest in my lord's whereabouts."

They stared at each other for a long moment before Lynman said, "I believe we understand one another, Lady Melford. Partially, that is. I must confess you puzzle me." He rose slowly, as if considering the matter. "You may give your husband a message for me, Lady Melford. You may tell him I have not forgotten." With these words, he turned and made for the door without a polite farewell as was customary.

For long moments after his departure, Nell sat as if turned to stone. What had he meant by his remark? she asked herself. He surely meant some harm to Andrew, she thought with trepidation. It must be prevented!

She paced the floor nervously until she heard Melford's voice in the hall. In a moment, the door opened and he was in the room with her. Nell refused to give in to her wild imagination (she told herself that was all it was) and greeted Lord Andrew with a smile. He dropped a kiss on her lips and went to the cupboard for a glass of wine.

When he was seated across from her, staring deeply into his glass, Nell said tentatively, "I had a visitor today, Andrew."

He glanced at her over the glass and said, "How nice. Was it someone I know?"

"Rather," she said firmly. "It was Viscount Lynman."

His face took on a stern mien and he asked with annoyance, "What is troubling you, Nell? Was the cad offensive?"

Nell frowned for a moment before saying, "I hardly know. He made me angry, and I rather tore into him." She smiled sheepishly.

Melford grinned, knowing what had happened. "Did it serve the purpose, my love?"

"I hardly know, Andrew. When he first came, he seemed determined to make love to me." She hastily reassured him when she saw his expression. "Don't upset yourself, Andrew. He never touched me. That is not what I meant. His tone is so complimentary and intimate that I feel constricted."

Andrew looked at her with narrowed eyes for a moment. "And then?" he asked with a tilt of his head. "There must be more."

Nell stared at her clasped hands for a long moment. "Well, you see, I didn't like him saying such things when I was alone, er . . . It was taking advantage of me, and—I did not like it. So, I started questioning him, and that was when he became offensive." She proceeded to tell him in detail of their conversation, finishing with, "And that was when he gave me the message for you."

"And what message was that, my dear?" Andrew asked slowly, considering her story in detail.

177

"It was innocuous enough. He said, 'Tell Melford that I have not forgotten.' He stalked from the room without another word." Nell ended dramatically.

A smothered oath came from the man sitting across from her, and she caught a steely glint in his eyes as they rested on her face. Nell crossed the room to stand beside his chair. Resting her hand on his shoulder, she asked, "What did he mean, Andrew?"

Melford stared into her eyes for a long, thoughtful moment before taking her hand into his. "Don't worry about this, my dear. I will deal with the situation. And Nell, I would rather you not receive the viscount when I am not present. Do you have any objection?" he asked questioningly.

Nell laughed and said, "Hardly. I have conceived a positive dislike for the gentleman." She hesitated. "Won't you tell me why the viscount is acting so oddly, Andrew?"

He shook his head firmly. "It is a story not fit for a lady's ears, and I have no intention of offending you with it. However, in the future I wish you to avoid the viscount."

Nell studied her clasped hands and said, "I am happy to obey you this time, Andrew."

"Meaning, I suppose, that you have no intention of obeying every order I give you," he commented with a grin.

She perched on his knee and said, "You know I would obey you in any serious matter, love."

He looked down at her with serious eyes and said, "I hope so, dearest," before drawing her tightly into his embrace.

They sat quietly together for some time before Nell finally asked, "Tired?"

He rubbed his cheek against her hair. "Pleasantly so, my dear. Though not too tired to love my tempting wife," he added with a lazy grin.

"I expected that sort of an answer," she retorted with a laugh.

"So you should," he said with such an intense look, that Nell jumped up and said, "Not now, my lord. It is nearly time to dress for dinner."

Andrew rose with a sigh and asked, "One kiss, then, my love. Surely you can spare one kiss for a tired husband?"

Nell permitted him to pull her back into his arms and enjoyed the passionate feel of his lips as they moved over her own. She melted into the world they shared each time they touched.

One morning, a few days later, Mrs. Thimble plunged the house into an orgy of what might have been termed spring cleaning, if only it were spring. Unfortunately, winter was very close by, and it was positively uncomfortable. Nell donned her cloak for a walk to escape the endless chatter of the maids as they turned the house upside down in their exertions.

She strolled toward the gazebo, remembering the last time she had walked in that direction, and felt a pang as she recalled her feelings on that occasion. Nell couldn't imagine anything more comfortable than the relationship she now shared with Melford.

The weeks had flown past since the hunting party had returned to their respective homes, and Nell had lived each to the fullest. Andrew was a wonderful lover, but there was more to him than his gentle lovemaking. He was a considerate husband, ever interested in her wishes. Nell loved him desperately.

She climbed up into the gazebo and seated herself

179

on the stone bench. It was chilly and she mustn't remain long, but she wanted a few moments alone. Not a room in the house was habitable after Mrs. Thimble had begun her twice yearly ritual. Melford had disappeared early in the morning, and Nell had not bothered to discover his direction.

She took a letter from Andrea out of the pocket of her cloak and opened it eagerly.

Dearest Nell,

I must write to find how you are faring now that your home is your own once more. I am certain you and Melford are happy to have the place to yourselves.

I am settled at Fairley for the winter with my dearest Elvira for company. It is not dreary, although I miss the company of my friends; you, dearest Nell, and your cousin, Caroline. I look forward to the season when we will be settled in London.

Give my regards to your husband, and if you should hear from Sir Henry Claymore, to him also. I long to hear from you, Nell, so please do answer as quickly as possible. With my sincerest regards,

Your friend,
A. Fairley

Nell folded the letter and tucked it back into her pocket as she considered the contents of the letter. Poor Andrea, all alone at her estate. Nell's heart went out to her, for she remembered how lonely she had been in the same situation.

Finally, she started slowly toward the house. It was of no earthly use to take cold from sitting outdoors, she told herself humorously.

When she entered the house, Thimble took her cloak and told her, "My lord is in the study, madam. He asked for you to join him when you returned."

Nell thanked him and, with a quick look in the glass to assure herself that she wasn't beyond redemption, hurried along to the study. Andrew was sitting at his desk when she entered the room, and he looked up briefly before saying, "I am writing to Harry, Nell."

"Oh? I received a letter from Lady Andrea this morning. She asks us to give her regards to Harry should we hear from him." As an afterthought, she added, "Oh, she sent her regards to you, also."

He grinned and said wryly, "Thank you, madam. I know how difficult it was for you to tell me that."

Nell flushed but refused to rise to the bait. "I just came in from a walk to the gazebo," she said. "It is coming on to snow again. I believe the weather is turning colder."

"Best stay inside. The wind is fierce on days like this." He returned to his letter to Harry.

Curiously, Nell stared at Andrew as he sat with his dark head bent over his letter and asked, "You haven't seen Viscount Lynman recently, I suppose?"

His head jerked up with a snap. "Why?"

She shrugged her shoulders. "No reason. I am curious. I keep wondering about his visit, and what he meant."

Melford dropped his letter to the desk and said firmly, "Stop thinking about it, Nell. It need not concern you. He most likely meant nothing. Do forget it."

"But Andrew, I feel certain he means to harm you," she said nervously. "I am certain of it."

He stood up and pulled her to her feet. Rocking her from side to side, he murmured into her ear, "Nell, Nell, Nell. Stop it! I won't have you worrying over me. He can't harm me, my love. Now promise you won't think of it again."

Nell showed him a strained face, but she forced a smile, and said, "I will try, Andrew."

He kissed her again and added, "Now that's a good girl. Don't fret over me, darling. I am not worth it."

She grinned and said, "You are to me."

They clung to each other for a long moment, and Nell wiped away a stubborn tear.

Chapter Twelve

The sun was peeking into the windows on this wintry morning as Nell woke from a sound sleep. She stretched sensuously beneath the warm covers and turned toward Andrew, whose back was toward her. Instinctively she put out her hand and slid her fingers over the hard muscles of his shoulder.

At her touch he woke and turned to face her, murmuring in a voice heavy with sleep, "Nell? Are you awake?"

Nell moved closer and allowed him to slip his arms around her and draw her into a warm embrace. "I couldn't sleep," she said. "I wonder why?"

His chuckle tickled her curls, and he said, "I am hoping."

Nell responded eagerly, "I'm willing."

His lips moved over her face, and he said, "I like your attitude, my girl. Don't ever change."

Nell surrendered to his gentle movements, and as his hands became more passionate, she let her own hands move over the planes of his back and shoulders, then move down over his firm hips. She whispered softly, "I love you, Andrew."

He drew in a ragged breath and answered, "So do I, darling. I could not live without you, Nell." He pulled her closer, and she willingly snuggled into his arms, letting his passion rouse her to the heights of fulfillment.

Later, they lay together with their arms wrapped around each other for a long, long time, exulting in their precious moment of intimacy. Before he went out for the day, Andrew came to the room where she was just completing her morning toilet and hugged her thoughtfully. Nell clung to him with an unusual urgency before she let him go.

The business of the day occupied her far more than usual. Nell approved the dinner menu with Mrs. Thimble and spoke with her maid about some repairs she wanted made to one of her gowns. She was about to go into the music room when a footman presented her with a note. She thanked him and opened it. It was very short and precise.

Nell,
Meet me at the edge of the garden behind the gazebo. I shall be waiting for you, my love.

Melford

She read it twice, wondering what it meant, but finally sent a footman for her cloak and bonnet. She donned them in the hall and told Thimble, "I am meeting my lord in the gardens. If he happens to

184

come in while I am out, that is where I shall be. I only tell you this in the event that I do not find him."

Taking her warm muff, she went out the back way and set off down the worn path. Her feet crunched on the snow, but very little other sound could be heard. She walked to the gazebo and looked around, but as she saw no sign of Melford, she continued on down the path toward the forest. A small frown creased her brow as she entered the wood, for she could not conceive of any reason why Melford should ask to meet her near the old cart track that led to the post road. At the edge of the forest a man stood with his back to her, and she rushed in his direction with a happy smile. "Darling, why did you . . . ?" she began when the man turned around and she saw that it was not Melford at all. It was Viscount Lynman!

His smile was unpleasant as he came toward her and said, "I am happy to see you are so prompt, my lady. It is a trifle cold today."

"What do you want with me, my lord?" Nell asked sternly. "As you say, it is cold out."

"No need to be so high in the instep with me, my lady," he said as he moved closer. "We are going to be very close for a time."

Taking fright, Nell tried to back away, at the same time asking in a scornful but frightened voice, "What do you mean, Lynman? I have no intention of becoming an intimate of yours!"

His laugh was harsh, and he grappled with her, pulling her closer. "You and I are taking a little journey, my lady. How does Scotland sound to you?" he asked with a hateful leer.

Nell began to struggle more fiercely. Something in

185

his voice told her that he was quite determined to have his way. She broke away for a moment, dropping her muff, but he caught her and bundled her into the closed carriage he had concealed behind the trees. He called loudly to the driver for help and in a moment she was inside.

Flung on the seat with no consideration for her dignity, Nell took only long enough to catch her breath, and scrambled for the other door. She knew only that he was taking her away from her beloved Andrew, and she had to do something in a hurry.

He caught her easily as she tried to jump from the doors of the now fast moving coach, and pulled her down beside him. He muttered, "I had hoped it would not be necessary to do this, my lady, but you force me." He pulled a flask from his coat pocket and said, "Drink."

Nell turned her head away, but he jerked it back and roughly forced the fiery liquid down her throat. The interior of the coach whirled around her, and before the blackness engulfed her completely, she said, "Melford will kill you for this."

When she awoke it was dark, although the coach continued to move, and she gingerly lifted her head from the seat. A grunt from the man on the other seat informed her that he was sleeping. Hope rose in her heart, and she shook her head, trying to clear it of the drug she had been forced to take. She righted herself slowly, and to her chagrin the viscount said, "Lie down again, my dear. We have a long distance to travel."

Nell leaned her head against the upholstered seat. It was swimming dreadfully. "Where are you taking me?" she asked fearfully.

"I told you earlier," he said, settling himself more comfortably on the cushions. "Accustom yourself. We are going to Scotland."

Nell's tongue was thick and her head swam, but she knew what a foolish proposition he was making. "It is nigh impossible to travel in this weather, sir. We will be killed."

He laughed. "Don't trouble yourself, my lady. We will be perfectly safe." He drew his coat more firmly around himself to keep out the cold. "Now, go to sleep, and no tricks. I am not above putting you to sleep once more if you cause me trouble," he told her brutally.

Nell closed her eyes, sickened at his rough voice. She thought of Andrew, and what he must be thinking. Tears filled her eyes, and she let them fall uninhibited down her cheeks. Her hand held tightly to the strap as the coach bounced and jolted over the ruts caused by the drifting snow. Finally, she fell into a fitful sleep.

Across from her, Lynman regarded her with a cynical smile. His plans were beginning to bear fruit. An old debt was being paid, and he intended to enjoy each installment of the payment.

When Nell woke several hours later, cold and shivering, the coach jolted her so badly she nearly fell from her precarious perch on the seat. Lynman was preparing to depart the carriage, but stopped to say, "If you have any notion of making a commotion, my lady, I advise you to forget it. And there is no need to try to leave a message for Melford. I have already informed him of our destination."

Nell gasped at his impudence before allowing him to assist her from the carriage. The landlord was told she had been ill, and she was solicitously shown to a room on the upper floor, where she threw off her cloak and immediately searched the room for a means of escape. Then caution told her she must discover what Lynman had meant by his last cryptic words to her. She would be able to leave him at another point on the road to Scotland.

Having so resolved, Nell looked into the glass, and was shocked at the ravages her rough treatment and grief had worn on her face. She opened the valise that had been brought to the room and inspected its contents. She was surprised to find that Lynman had considered her every need. She found two traveling gowns and many toilet articles even her particular scent. Her kidnapper was a discerning gentleman, she thought cynically.

She poured water into the bowl and began to wash her face and arms. Despite the snow on the ground, she was covered with a fine film of grime. While brushing her hair until it shone, she let her mind busily explore all avenues of escape. When at last she could find no other excuse for remaining in her room, she repacked her valise carefully, before returning to the private parlor where Lynman waited impatiently.

He rose at her entrance, surprising Nell so much that she halted in the doorway to stare at him in shock. He looked approvingly at her and said, "I see you made use of the things I brought for you. I felt certain I could depend on you to come around in the end."

Nell entered the room and closed the door with a snap. "I haven't come around in the least, my lord. I don't happen to be a fool, however, and I know it would look very singular if I journeyed the length of England wearing the same untidy gown, and I am stunned at your unnecessary politeness."

He roared with laughter and asked, "Do you think it would be less singular if you are dressed up to the nines? What a charmingly refreshing point of view," he added as he seated her at the dinner table.

"Nothing could make this journey less singular, my lord. Perhaps you feel able to inform me of the necessity for it?" she asked coldly.

He shook his head. "Your husband will know, and that is all I require, Nell. I sent him a note informing him of your desire to join me at my hunting lodge in Scotland," he said with relish.

Nell replaced her fork on the table and said scornfully, "How foolish of you, Viscount. I was almost beginning to respect your intellect." She took a deep breath and continued, "Why, Melford will be on the road as soon as he receives your message."

He laughed and gestured to the food. "Eat up, my dear. I am perfectly well aware of that fact. And he will worry every step of the way. He will wonder about you, and what I am doing with you."

Nell's chin shot up. "Oh, you loathsome creature!" she cried out bitterly. "I will escape from you if it is the last thing I do!"

He bit into his steak with relish. "Why do that? Melford will be along after you sooner or later."

Nell planted her eyes on her food and refused to reply or lift them again for the remainder of the meal. Her mind worked furiously. She would make this creature sorry if it was the last thing she did! she told herself furiously.

Nell stepped willingly into the coach when they

resumed their journey later. Nothing would be gained by escape. She would bide her time until Melford caught up with them. Then this odious creature would be made to see sense. She occupied herself with thinking up outrageous means of punishment for him. Boiling in oil was too good for someone as vile as Lynman had proved himself to be.

Nell eventually tired of her silence. It was extremely boring, so she turned to Lynman speculatively. She wondered if he happened to have a pistol with him. She had not noticed one earlier.

Lynman saw her considering expression and asked, "Now what are you plotting, my lady? Be assured that you will never succeed."

Nell lifted her chin and asked, "Why should I be plotting anything? You have said that my husband will rescue me, so why should I worry?" She gave him a cold, biting look.

He laughed with delight. "You are all innocence, milady, but I am well aware that if you can escape me before Melford comes, you will. But let me tell you this, Nell. After the next few days, even Melford won't want you. He will never believe that we have not been lovers," he said with a scornful laugh.

Color flamed into Nell's cheeks and she said, "You underestimate the power of our attraction, milord; Melford will not think such a thing for I will tell him differently. He will believe me." Her green eyes glowed angrily and her back was straight as she spit her words at him.

He shrugged and said, "Believe what you will, madam. It is all one to me. However, we shall see what we shall see."

"You are despicable. Why should you want to

harm me? I barely know you!" she cried out in exasperation.

Delighted by her spirit, he willingly took part in the ensuing discussion. "My dearest lady," he said. "I haven't the slightest desire to harm you. Indeed, I feel, ever so slightly, mind you, a definite partiality for you."

Nell flushed again and said, "May I say that I do not have any partiality for you, slight or otherwise?"

He laughed and waited for the outburst that was sure to come.

Nell clenched her teeth and asked, "You have not told me the reason for this scandalous abduction, my lord. Do you mean to do so?"

He shrugged and stared out the window, angering her fiercely. Several moments passed and there was deep silence broken only by the blowing of the horses and the swearing of the coachmen at the cold.

Then Lynman said, "I have naught against you, Lady Melford. However, your husband and I have an old score to settle and I mean to take care of it. Now be satisfied with that, ma'am, for I don't mean to tell you more."

His expression was so fierce that Nell subsided in frightened silence. What had he meant, she wondered fleetingly. Nell remembered Andrew telling her of an old score between them. Something not fit for the ears of a lady, he had said.

Her curiosity was now piqued, and she wondered about it during the long, cold ride until lunchtime. Nell joined Lynman for the meal, albeit rather wearily. It had been so long since she had seen her bed that she was scarcely able to walk.

That night when they stopped at the inn, Nell

hardly remembered what she ate, she was so tired. All thoughts of fleeing left her mind when she saw the bed waiting for her.

Although exhausted, she slept only fitfully, her dreams full of Andrew. In the darkest hours before dawn, she fell into a deep, dreamless sleep that brought forgetfulness. When she woke early in the morning, she turned over in bed, reaching for the comfort of Melford's arms, only to waken to hateful reality. Everything came back to her in a rush. She lay on her stomach with clenched fingers, hoping to still the forceful longing for her husband. Sobs threatened to engulf her, but she managed to choke them down and later to dress and face another long day of traveling.

Her face was wan and peaked when she joined Lynman for breakfast, and he wondered for a moment if she were going to be ill. That would make things awkward, he thought with irritation! He felt a remote pang for her distress, but he would not let it deter him. He meant to even the score with Melford once and for all.

Nell ate her breakfast without speaking. She had barely finished her meal when an acute feeling of nausea struck her, and she excused herself hastily. Rushing to her chamber, she promptly lost her breakfast in the chamber pot. She fell limply across the bed for several moments, not taking notice when Lynman entered the room after a brief knock.

He watched her for a short time, then said, "What sort of trick are you up to, madam? We must be on our way."

Nell gasped. "I am not well, sir. I am *sorry* to be *such* a bother!" she said sarcastically.

He grinned and said, "I'll wager you are. Come madam, we must be off at once, or do you have a desire to remain at this inn?"

She asked eagerly, "What do you mean?"

"Not what you seem to think, my lady." He sighed. "It appears to be coming on to snow outside. I don't believe you would enjoy being snowbound here with me."

Nell tried unsuccessfully to suppress a shudder. "God forbid!" she said. Allowing him to help her to her feet, she stood meekly while he placed the cloak around her shoulders.

He supported her down the stairs and into the carriage with the suitable expressions of concern. Once away from prying eyes, he said, "You may cut line, Nell. I am not impressed."

Nell looked at him with angry eyes. "You may force me to travel with you, my lord, but it is not within your power to command my bodily functions. Be assured that I would make myself well, were it possible. I have no desire to be dependent upon you for my concerns," she said scathingly.

"What has made you ill?" he asked firmly. "You were in perfect health last evening."

"No doubt it is due to your forced company, my lord. When I am able to look my last upon you, I have no doubt I shall revive wonderfully," she said scornfully.

"Talking will not mend matters," he replied. "I could make things much more uncomfortable for you," he threatened.

Nell closed her eyes and leaned her weary head against the squabs of the chaise. "I suppose you might," she agreed, "if you enjoy making love to a female who must hang over a chamber pot or out the windows of the coach."

Revolted, he stared at her without renewing the conversation. He must reconsider. Was she really ill? He had no way of knowing. Of a certainty the little countess would bear watching! She had more strength of character than he would have believed, he thought with admiration.

Once during the afternoon Nell opened her eyes and asked, "How long until we reach Scotland?"

He grunted and said, "The journey usually takes four days."

Nell stared at him for a long moment, then asked with asperity, "Could you not have found a place nearby? I am certain I could be ruined in half the time."

He laughed heartily and said, "I'm sure you could be ruined in one fraction of that time, ma'am." He hesitated before saying, "It is not my intention to ruin you, my lady. No one other than Melford knows of our little tryst."

Nell watched him for a moment. "If you don't mean to ruin me, what exactly are your intentions?"

"I told you last evening. I am determined to repay an old debt to Melford. He will worry about you. As the days pass, it will become worse and worse for him. When he finds us, he will be so wild that his judgement will be off. He will challenge me to a duel and when he does, I intend to kill him," he concluded brutally.

Nell listened in horror as he calmly stated his intentions, and knew that she must somehow stop him from fulfilling his wish. She murmured, "You are despicable, Lynman. Certainly, you are no gentleman."

He laughed and said, "Tell me something I do *not* know, ma'am."

Day followed weary day, and the cold increased as they journeyed further north. Each morning, Nell felt a recurrence of the nausea that had affected her on that first morning at the inn, but it was never so severe, and she was able to control it. She was extremely puzzled and not able to account for her illness, for travel had never made her unwell in the past. She reasoned it must have something to do with her newly wedded state. She smiled ruefully. Her body was not quite as it had been before she had lived with Melford.

Lynman was as polite as ever, treating her with the respect her station demanded. If it had not been for Melford's absence, she could have imagined herself to be on a pleasant journey. It was only when she dared to mention Melford that he became angry with her, though he never became violent. Nell agonized over her knowledge of his intentions. She knew she would never let him murder her husband, and so decided to remain with him at least until they reached Scotland. He never locked her in her chamber, and she had no doubt she could contrive something when they came to the hunting lodge he spoke of. Keeping her own counsel, she remained docilely with him, lulling him with her complaisance.

Lynman was becoming curious. Lady Melford had taken her situation with startling aplomb. He fully intended to harm her husband, and had left her in no doubt of the situation, yet she showed no sign of fear, or even regret. What could she possibly be thinking of? he wondered.

Nell's thoughts wound from one extreme to another. One moment she was reasonably content, then she would plunge to the depths. It was something she had never experienced before, these sudden changes in mood, but she put it down to the forced travel in such inclement weather.

The countryside had been changing during the past days, and the bare, bleak Scottish countryside became more and more familiar. The accent of the people changed to the harsh Scots brogue, and Nell knew it was time for her to plan her escape from the viscount.

Nell knew Andrew could not be so far behind them. If she wanted to help him, she could not remain one day beyond their arrival at the hunting lodge. If Melford were to arrive at the lodge, she would not place it above Lynman to murder him in cold blood.

Chapter Thirteen

On the afternoon that Nell was captured, Melford rode lazily toward the Chase from the main gates. It had been a hard day, and he was feeling particularly worn. It would be comforting to sit with Nell and let her softness drive the chill from his body. At the front door, he tossed the reins to a groom and ran lightly up the steps, removing his gloves and great-coat as he walked toward the library, where Nell usually waited for him.

He tossed his outer garments onto a small chair in the hall and entered the library, slamming the door after him. Surprised to find the room empty he rang the bell and poured himself a glass of wine from the decanter stored in the cupboard.

Thimble entered noiselessly. "You rang, my lord?"

Melford smiled at his old ally and said, "Yes, Thimble. Have my lady join me here, if you please."

Thimble's old eyes widened in surprise. "I am

afraid that is impossible, my lord. She is not at home. I would have thought . . ." he broke off, realizing that he had no right stating his thoughts to the master of the house.

Lord Melford stared at Thimble with curiosity. Something was obviously bothering the old man. "Of course she is home, Thimble," Melford said. "Where would she have gone at this time of day?"

Thimble cleared his throat nervously. "My lord, Lady Melford went to meet you in the gardens earlier. To my knowledge she has not returned."

Melford swallowed all the amber liquid in his glass in a gulp. "Let us begin again, Thimble. I haven't the slightest guess as to what you are saying."

"To the best of my knowledge," Thimble began, "Lady Melford received a note, purported to be from yourself, sir, asking her to meet you in the gardens. She left a message with a footman, telling you to meet her there if she happened to miss you."

Melford absently poured another glass of brandy and sat down in a chair by the fire. "I sent no note, Thimble. What time was this?"

"I have no way of knowing exactly, my lord," said Thimble. "It was definitely before luncheon."

Melford stared at the liquid in his glass, an unaccustomed feeling of anxiety gathering in his stomach. He drew in a ragged breath and said, "We will not immediately assume anything is amiss, Thimble. Have someone go up to the master suite and see if anything is missing. If my lady is there, inform me. Also, have someone search the gardens. I will wait for your answer."

Thimble left the library, only to return in a very

few moments. "I was in the process of carrying out your orders, my lord, when a lad from the stables brought a note for you. He refused to give it into my hand. May I bring him in?"

Melford's eyes lit up and he said, "Yes, of course, Thimble. Perhaps he can help us solve this riddle."

The boy came into the room with his hat in his hands and said, "'Ere's your note, me lord. I wuz told to gie it into yer hand, and no other." He gave a defiant look at Thimble.

Melford took the note and asked, "Who gave it to you, lad?"

"Don't know, me lord. A great swell, he wuz. A Lunnon gen'lman what said he had ta git a note ta yer ludship. I took the note. I hope I done right, me lord?"

Melford slipped a coin into his waiting hand and said, "You did just the right thing, lad. Thank you. That will be all."

When the boy had gone, Melford said, "I want my curricle brought round in thirty minutes, Thimble. And have my valet pack a few things for me. Whatever is in this note, I will be off immediately."

Thimble stared into his eyes for a long moment, then said, "I hope you find her ladyship, sir. All the staff are concerned for her safety."

Melford smiled at the old man and added, "Thank you, Thimble. I hope we can keep this story to ourselves. Her ladyship's good name depends upon it."

Thimble smiled and said, "Never fear, sir. All the staff are that fond of my lady. They would lie themselves blue in the face before letting a word of this story get about."

When Thimble left him alone, Melford sank into the seat near the fire. With a trembling hand he opened the letter and began to read.

My dear Melford,

It brings me great pleasure to inform you that Lady Melford has elected to accompany me to my lodge in Scotland. It will be of no avail to follow, for we will be long on our journey when you receive this note.

She sends you her most sincere regrets and hopes you will understand her choice.

With Pleasure,
Gerard Fordyce, Viscount Lynman

The end of the letter brought forth a bout of swearing that did not stop for many long moments.

When Thimble informed Melford that his curricle was at the door, he put on his hat, coat, and gloves and hurried out. He told him, "Don't expect to hear from me soon. I will be some time on the road. I will send a message when I have recovered her ladyship."

He ran out to the waiting carriage, found his groom sitting up behind, and took the reins. The curricle made much better time than a cumbersome coach, and they were in London by ten o'clock the next morning after a long cold ride through the burgeoning snow. Melford stopped at his town house for a change of clothing and breakfast. Welby welcomed him warmly, informing him that breakfast would be served shortly.

Lord Melford sat tiredly in the study. He sent a note round to St. James Street in the hopes that Sir

Harry had arrived the previous week from his estates.

He had just sat down at the breakfast table when Sir Harry arrived, and he joined him at table. When both were comfortably situated with full plates, Harry said, "What has brought you up to town in weather like this, Andrew? It must be some weighty matter."

Melford's face was drawn and weary from the long night of driving. "There *is* something wrong, Harry. Believe it or not, that damned Lynman has abducted Nell."

He tossed the letter to Harry while he tucked into his food. Harry's mouth dropped open in surprise. Gathering his wits about him, he opened the letter and read it through to the finish. Then he dropped it to the table and absentmindedly began to eat. Finally he said, "I understood you to say that he abducted her. The letter hardly reads that way."

Melford gave him a vicious look and said, "I don't give a damn how that blasted letter sounds, Harry! He abducted her, I say!" His fist smashed down onto the table.

Harry hid a smile and said, "I don't mean to upset you, dear boy, but you hardly seemed on the best of terms with her when I stayed with you. You don't think . . ."

"No, I don't think any such thing, Harry. It is true that everything was not as it should have been, but that was worked out. That fiend has taken her off, and I intend to see to it that he pays for it!" Melford cried out savagely.

Harry relented. "When do we leave?"

Andrew grinned. "I knew I could depend on you, Harry. I mean to be on my way as soon as possible."

They completed their meal in a hurry and Harry left with a casual wave of his hand. Melford promised to call in St. James Street in under an hour. It was just on the hour when Melford rode down the street at a strict trot, having just completed several errands. Harry was on the lookout for him, and had his portmanteau up in the carriage in a trice. Soon the friends were on their way out of London on the Great North Road.

The cold wind whipped around them as the horses galloped at a full pace from the city, and for a time no sound could be heard other than the noise of the city and the horses' hooves on the muddy road. Then Harry said, "I suppose that affair in Venice is behind this caper."

Andrew shook his head. "I have considered the matter all night and I can come to no other conclusion. You must be right."

With their thoughts turned inward, they traveled on through the day. Harry was concerned for Melford and Nell, of whom he had grown fond. Harry had never seen Melford so wild before, and he very much feared that he would see him commit mayhem before this crazy adventure was over. He said unthinkingly, "You know, Andrew, that Lynman has had plenty of time to, umm, er, take her, I suppose?"

His only reply was a groan and, "Oh, God, Harry! Do you think I haven't thought about it every moment since I found her missing?"

Harry cleared his throat and said, "I'm sorry, old chap. I don't know what made me say such a thing. Wasn't thinking." He hunched down into his coat and occupied his time figuring the distance they had traveled.

Melford tensely whipped up his horses in reaction to Harry's comment.

They inquired after the couple at every toll gate and inn they passed and found that they were many hours behind them. Melford was encouraged to know that he and Harry were on the right track and wanted to push on even harder, but Harry urged caution. When they paused for dinner, Harry spoke up. "Andrew, I have been thinking."

Andrew cried out in mock horror, "Oh, my God! What could have induced you to do that?"

Harry replied with a wry grin, "No need to be offensive, Andrew. Listen to me. I don't believe you have anything to fear with regard to that unfortunate remark I made earlier."

"Oh? What makes you think so?"

"It is really very simple, Andrew. I wonder you had not thought of it yourself. I believe he wants you to think exactly what you *have* been thinking. The man is not that far gone to all gentlemanly practices, you must admit," he said reasonably.

Andrew shook his head adamantly. "I admit no such thing. I have not forgotten how he tried to seduce the daughter of one of my respected acquaintances when we were in Venice, and another time he did something similar when we met in the East. Any man who would perpetrate such a caper is a complete bounder." Harry did not speak and Melford thought about his theory for some time before adding, "Did you really mean that, Harry?"

"Of course. Everything points to it. Take that letter, for instance." He shook his head wisely. "It is too

203

obvious if you look at it objectively. You must see that."

"I am not able to look at it objectively, Harry," Andrew said bluntly. "Explain."

Harry held his fork poised in midair and pointed it at Andrew. "In the first place, you don't write a letter nicely calculated to send a man flying like a bull at a red handkerchief, and then go one further and give him your direction. It just ain't done." He wagged his head wisely.

"Besides, man," Harry continued, "this is Britain. Whatever standards may hold in Europe or the East do not hold here! He could never get away with it. To ruin Nell would surely mean his own social destruction, for you have too many friends who would stand behind you."

Andrew stared at him for a long thoughtful moment before saying, "You could be right, Harry."

Harry laughed scornfully. "Of course I am! Only an idiot or a fool in love would have missed it. He wanted you to think Nell was eloping with him. He would have succeeded if you and Nell hadn't come to an understanding before this bit of devilry."

Andrew drained his wineglass in one gulp. "You know, Harry, it will be wonderful if I don't strangle that scoundrel with my bare hands when we do catch up with him."

"Don't blame you in the least, dear boy. Would feel just the same if it was my wife," Harry said sympathetically.

Melford sighed with fatigue. "I don't believe we should try to push on tonight, Harry. I am dead on my feet, and can hardly think straight." They bespoke rooms for the night, and Melford climbed wearily up to his bed, where he tossed fitfully. Dreams of Nell interrupted his rest and his mind played tricks on him. Nearly falling asleep, he would find his body would jerk and he would be fully awake once more.

They were on the road at first light after a frugal breakfast. He promised Harry they would stop in the middle of the day for a large luncheon to make up for the loss of his morning refreshment. They made good time, although they continued to stop at each tollgate for information concerning the missing pair.

When evening came, they were pleased at their progress and stopped at an inn, where they bespoke dinner and beds. When they were seated in their private parlor Harry asked, "Do you know the location of this hunting lodge of Lynman's?" He idly swirled the liquid in his glass.

Andrew lit a cigar and said, "I don't think there will be any difficulty in the matter, Harry. He should be well known in the district. I have heard that he makes a practice of spending time there each year."

"In that eventuality he should be well known. With his reputation it won't be hard to locate him," Harry said with certainty.

"I believe you must be foxed, Harry. That is what I just said," Andrew said with a laugh.

"No, no!" Harry disclaimed. "I am fully well able to hold my liquor," he cried in outraged dignity. "You should know that by now."

For a lighthearted moment, Andrew laughed and said, "I apologize, dear boy. I wouldn't insult your prowess with the bottle for anything in the world.

After several days on the road without catching up with Nell and her abductor, Harry was tired and

Andrew more angry than ever. When they halted for the evening, Melford was in a black mood and spoke very little. Harry held his peace, knowing the only thing to bring his friend any respite would be the sight of his beloved Nell.

Dinner was a silent meal, unbroken except for the words of the footmen as they brought in the food and changed the courses. They retired soon after, hoping for an early start on the morrow.

Something happened during the night that changed all their plans. The snow that had been falling lightly during the day began to blanket the earth in its tender caress. No one could get through the drifting snowbanks that had formed on the roads. When morning came, it was impossible to leave the inn. They were forced to face the possibility that it would be days, maybe a week, before they would be able to travel again.

Chapter Fourteen

Nell and the viscount arrived at his hunting lodge the evening before the weather had made travel impossible for Melford and Sir Harry. The snow continued to fall as she descended from the carriage, and Lynman hurried Nell into the great hall where his butler greeted them politely.

Coldly ignoring the servant's words, Lynman said, "I expect to be in residence for some time, and the Countess of Melford will be my guest." He led the way into the drawing room where a warm fire was waiting for them, before seating himself carelessly, without waiting for Nell to do so.

He looked at her coldly and said, "Sit down, my lady, and be comfortable. You are free to do what you will in my house, for unless I miss my guess, it is coming on to snow again and the roads will soon be impassable. I believe you are far too sensible to attempt to escape under these circumstances."

Nell seated herself near the fire. "You are perfectly

right, milord. You may rely on my good sense. How long will we be snowbound?" she asked.

He shrugged his shoulders inconsiderately. "Who can tell?" he asked. "Perhaps a day or so, then maybe a week."

Nell was appalled but attempted to keep this from showing on her face. She had no desire to offer him the opportunity to amuse himself at her expense.

Several days passed and the weather showed no signs of letting up. Nell became impatient with her quiet existence, and she could see that Lynman was becoming distracted, too. She remained to herself for the most part, only seeing the viscount at mealtime. He did not try to force her to entertain him, and Nell was grateful he showed her that much kindness under the circumstances. The fire crackled in the hearth as Nell prowled listlessly about the dimly lit sitting room. The overcast sky made the house appear to be sleeping.

Anxiety rode Nell's shoulder as she went down to the library to search for something to divert her agonized mind. She picked up a volume of sermons, and dropped wearily into a large wing chair situated cozily near the fire. She stared into the flames and imagined she could see Melford's likeness staring back at her. A tear trickled down her cheek. How had he reacted to her disappearance? Had he believed the wicked note Lynman had sent him? Or had he instinctively known it for what it was?

Nell's heart smote her as she thought of Andrew hating her. How could he ever believe she had not gone willingly? She *had* invited Lynman's attentions when they had first met in London, she remembered distractedly.

Now a new devil leered at her. Lynman had stated positively that Melford would never believe that he, Lynman, had not taken her. He had laughed at her distress, saying patronizingly, "Oh, little Nell. You must forget your dear Melford. He won't have you now."

Nell had answered with pride, "He will never believe such a thing for I will tell him differently."

Lynman had stared at her enigmatically and said, "I could make it the truth, my lady. Remember, you are alone with me in this place. No one would attempt to stop me if I chose to do so."

Nell's fury had known no bounds. She had informed him angrily, "You may succeed in doing such a thing, Viscount. I am but a mere female, and my strength cannot compare with yours. However, be warned. If you should dare to do such a thing, it will not be necessary for Melford to avenge me, for I will murder you myself long before he arrives."

Nell trembled anew as she recalled his face. He had dissolved into laughter that had not abated for several moments. Then he said, "As a matter of interest, how would you accomplish such a feat?"

Nell had sniffed in disdain. "You are not at all particular about your firearms, my lord. It would be no great feat to borrow one for the purpose."

He had laughed heartily at the jest, not for one moment considering it a real possibility. It was common knowledge that no female could bear the noise of a gun, much less use one.

Nell remembered that moment in her fury. She had refused to speak further on the subject, although he had not stopped twitting her at every meeting.

She dropped the book unopened, to look out the

209

tall windows at the far end of the room. Nell pulled open the shutters to stare into the whiteness of the winter day, and knew that somehow she must get away from him. How could it be done with the snow holding her inside so completely? It would not be feasible to go out into the snow, for death would surely follow as she would certainly be lost within moments of leaving the lodge. She barely remembered the direction to the main road south and toward the safety of her home. Of one thing Nell was determined. She must arm herself at the earliest opportunity for she had no intention of allowing Lynman the chance of taking advantage of her. With a pistol in her hands, she would be safe from his attentions.

Nell considered the matter. Earlier she had found a gun case in the study, and it was but the work of a moment to discover that it was not locked. A soft rustle sounded in the hallway and Nell moved from the case. It was not safe to do this now, but she decided to come back during the night when everyone was sleeping.

That night when Nell came down to dinner, no inkling of her intentions could be seen in her face. Lynman was as courteous as ever, but the smirk of a smile told her that his civility was not very deep and only a small jolt could push him over the line.

She kept up a running commentary of social chit-chat but soon discovered he had no intention of conversing with her. At the end of the meal he started baiting her again when he accompanied her in the library.

He leaned back, glass in hand, and said curiously, "I wonder where Melford is staying at this moment.

In this weather it is too much to hope that he could get through."

Nell folded her hands in her lap and stared stubbornly into the fire. She had no intention of showing him her discomfort. The only sign of her agitation was in her flaming eyes, and they were carefully averted from him.

He took a sip from his glass and tried again. "It will be somewhat amusing to inform Melford of our pleasure during the last weeks." He stared down into the amber-colored liquid and gave a sigh of purely malicious pleasure. "How I shall enjoy my revenge, my lady! It is perfect."

Nell turned at that point to give him a look of violent distaste. She rose to her feet and said, "If you will excuse me, I will retire for the night. I find I have no taste for this discussion."

He laughed and said, "Aye, go. It will do you no good, ma'am. No good at all. I have arranged your future. Got everything all right and tight, by now. Oh, yes."

His laughter followed her from the room as she marched stiffly to the door, her back ramrod straight. Nell didn't stop until her chamber door resounded smartly behind her. She turned the key in the lock and only then did she dare to draw a deep sigh.

Nell paced the floor for long hours, trying to come to the right decision. What to do? What to do? was the singsong refrain that circled round and round in her head.

She considered the possibilities. The servants were her only hope, and Nell considered each of them in turn. She dismissed the stable hands immediately. They would inform Lynman at the first inkling of an

211

approach for help. The maids were in no position to help her, so the only possibility was the housekeeper. The outlook hardly seemed promising, and Nell was beginning to fear for herself. What would Lynman do to her if Melford never came? Would he cast her out penniless? She hardly thought so, but could not be certain. He seemed evil enough for anything.

At last she made up her mind to approach the housekeeper as soon as it was feasible. If one must depend upon oneself, then one must be resigned, she thought dejectedly.

Nell woke slowly the next morning. As had become the norm during the last days, she was promptly sick. The strange nausea had continued after the journey ended and Nell could find no reason for it. Soon she was feeling more the thing and rose slowly. She still felt queasy as she put on her gown, but she determined to follow through with her plans for the morning. It seemed more urgent every moment, though Nell could hardly guess why.

When she was dressed, she walked down to the kitchens, where she found the housekeeper talking with the cook, and stopped near the door. She knew that most cooks were possessive about their kitchens, and so she waited patiently until they finished their discussion.

When Mrs. Pemberton became aware of her presence in the room, she turned to Nell with a wary smile. "Good morning, my lady. Is there aught I can do for you?"

Nell offered her most placating smile and said, "If you have a moment I would like to speak privately with you, Mrs. Pemberton."

A trifle plump, Mrs. Pemberton puffed from the

room, saying with a brusque look on her chubby face, "I have a few moments, ma'am. My room is right in here."

Nell followed her and took the offered seat. "Now, my lady, what can I do for you?" Mrs. Pemberton asked.

Nell gave her an open smile and began, "I will be honest with you, ma'am. I need your help very much. I hope you can help me."

The dour Scotswoman warmed under her gentle smile and said, "I hope I can be of help to ye, my lady. What is it?"

"I want to go away from here. I must return to my home. Could you possibly help me?" Nell asked her bluntly. She felt that prevarication would not serve in this instance.

Mrs. Pemberton looked at her for a long time before saying, "I don't know, milady. It would be hard." She looked Nell over sternly and added, "And in your condition, ma'am, you should not be jaunter-ing about in that way."

Nell's eyes opened wide. "What do you mean? What condition?"

Mrs. Pemberton laughed again and asked, "When is the child due to be born, milady? It is obvious to anyone with eyes in his head."

In an instant Nell realized what she should have known all along! What a fool she had been, she thought happily, before everything came rushing back to her in force. She still had to leave Lynman behind. She said, "I am not perfectly certain, but I don't think I can be very far along."

The woman smiled kindly and said, "Why don't

you wait for the arrival of Lord Melford, milady? Surely that would be best?"

Nell recalled the story Lynman had spun upon their arrival, and she said with perfect truth, "When my lord arrives, ma'am, he will not be in the best of spirits. He may duel with Lord Lynman. You see, the viscount abducted me. I am being held here by force until my husband's arrival."

The good woman was properly horrified by Nell's story and said at last, "I might be able to help you, but have you any money?"

Nell shook her head. "No, I didn't have my reticule with me," she said. Then an idea came to mind. "Where does the viscount keep his money, ma'am?"

Mrs. Pemberton was shocked and said, "You would not consider taking it by stealth, my lady!"

Nell's face hardened. "Mrs. Pemberton, I mean to leave this place one way or another. Lord Lynman stole me away from my husband with a lying note. He means to ruin my marriage for no more than a whim that I can see. I do not know at this moment if my husband will have me back, or if he will believe the lies your master sent to him. I would not hesitate to take my fare home from his coffers, ma'am."

The woman stared into Nell's face for a long moment. She searched her expression and saw the honesty deep in her eyes. "I will help you, my lady. It will be no problem about the money. I am able to put my hand on considerable sums put by for housekeeping expenses. He will never notice the loss."

Nell exclaimed happily, but the woman continued, "It will be another day before you can leave, milady. The road will be passable tomorrow. I will get the

214

money for you. Be ready before daylight in the morning with your valise packed. If you will come to the side door, one of the stable boys will take you to the stagecoach in the village. I'll see to't he stays till the coach leaves with ye inside. Now, don't fret, ma'am. It will be all right. Today you must rest, for the journey won't be like riding in a private carriage."

Nell couldn't keep the tears from flowing freely, and she impulsively threw her arms around the lady and planted a grateful kiss on her plump cheek. Mrs. Pemberton clucked disapprovingly and sent her to the breakfast parlor for her breakfast.

The room was empty, and Nell could only be thankful. She feared it would be nigh impossible to hide her joy at the knowledge that it would be only a short time until she was free from Lynman's oppressive presence.

Nell took Mrs. Pemberton's advice and rested during the afternoon. By successful maneuvering, she managed to avoid the viscount until dinner time. She was dressed for the occasion as usual with her meager wardrobe, and he smiled warmly when she came into the room.

"You are looking lovelier than ever, my lady," he said in something of the manner he had used in the beginning of their acquaintance.

Nell stared coldly back at him and said, "I know how I may take that, my lord."

He looked puzzled but refrained from other such remarks. He seated her solicitously at the table. "You have kept yourself busy today, Lady Melford," he remarked courteously.

Nell remained cold to him and said, "One does accustom oneself after a time to anything, my lord."

215

Her coldness stopped his pretence at politeness and he said, "This attitude won't mend matters, ma'am. Why won't you make the best of things?"

Unable to eat upon hearing this remark, she replaced her fork on the table and without regard for the servants said, "Lord Lynman, it would not matter if Melford were to throw me into the streets when he reaches this place. I would still not accept overtures from you."

He looked furious, but continued to eat his dinner with complacence. "You will sing a different tune when it happens," he sneered. "Then we will see."

Nell's eyes flashed and she said coldly, "You have yet to convince me that Melford will believe your version of that story, Lynman." She would never let him see her agony of spirit.

He laughed maliciously. "He'll believe it. I do have a reputation which is well deserved. He knows me from long past. He will believe me when I tell him that you have been with me willingly from the beginning."

Every word he uttered pierced Nell to the quick, but she refused to give him the satisfaction of seeing her pain. "You underestimate my husband's good sense, Viscount. As you said, he knows you well and he will know that you took me by force. I fear he will kill you. Yes," she added thoughtfully, "if you make your boasts to Melford, he will surely kill you."

He laughed and said, "Never think it. I am his match with either swords or pistols, my lady. Chance may favor myself."

"I am afraid that we must agree to disagree, my lord, as this discussion appears about to dissolve into a quarrel," Nell said complacently.

When Nell rose at the end of the meal, Lynman followed her into the library saying, "I will have my port with you, ma'am. It has been a damned boring day, all told. I believe you can provide entertainment of sorts," he added with an attempt at lightness.

"I am certain it won't be up to your usual standard, my lord," Nell replied.

He absently filled his glass. "The roads should be open soon. We will see Melford within the next few days. Then we shall see sport."

"If you think he will believe me to be your willing accomplice, why do you think he will come for me?" Nell asked curiously.

He laughed and said, "If you don't know the answer to that, I have no intention of enlightening you."

Nell sniffed and stared into the flames. This is becoming a habit, she thought ruefully as she glared into the fire.

Somehow, the evening passed and soon it was time to retire for the night. Nell thankfully made her escape from the dark room and Lynman's depressing presence. She leaned quietly against the closed door in her room for a long moment with bated breath and pounding heart. She started to pack her valise, but decided to wait until morning as she had so few garments to take with her.

Nell slept fitfully and was awake early in the morning. She swiftly packed her things and put on her cloak and bonnet. Then, carrying the valise, she tiptoed into the corridor, nervously stepping over the loose floorboard at the head of the stairs.

Mrs. Pemberton was waiting at the foot of the stairs when Nell came down and took the valise from

217

Nell with a frown. "Let me take that, my lady. You must have a care for yourself."

She led Nell into the kitchen, where she served her a breakfast of buttered bread and eggs in the firelit room. When she finished eating, Nell followed her outside to the waiting gig. Mrs. Pemberton placed a purse filled with money into her hand and said, "Here is enough money to take you on the stage, or mebbe you can hire a chaise, milady. I don't rightly know what the charges should be."

Nell accepted the purse with murmured thanks to the old woman, then climbed into the gig, where a boy had taken the reins into his hands. Mrs. Pemberton added, "Never fear, milady. The roads are still bad, but Dougal knows the lane like the back of his hand and you won't get lost. He will stay with you until you are off."

"Thank you again, Mrs. Pemberton." Nell hesitated and then added, "If Lord Melford comes, please tell him what I have done."

The plump old woman nodded her head once more, then went back into her warm kitchen. Dougal took up the reins and they were off. The wind blew strongly from the north and it was horribly cold. Yet Nell bore the discomfort without complaint. She was far too happy about her apparent escape to complain about her mode of travel. She wondered about the purse the housekeeper had given her. Would she be able to hire a carriage or would she be forced to take the common stage? She felt sick this morning as usual and she hoped she could control the nausea until she reached the inn.

After an eternity, Dougal turned the gig abruptly and Nell found herself in the inn yard of the little village. She descended with Dougal's help and was grateful for the support of his presence while she made her arrangements.

The landlord, a burly man, looked Nell over with a jaundiced eye when she demanded a room and chaise, but he commanded his men to do her bidding. He quoted her the charges and was surprised when she paid up immediately before following the maid to the chamber at the end of the hallway.

Nell had reason to be thankful to Mrs. Pemberton, she found when she reached the privacy of her room. She opened the purse and was surprised to find that after paying for the chamber and the chaise, thirty pounds yet remained. More than enough to see to the journey home.

She took most of the money and bound it into her handkerchief and tied it under her chemise for safety. The remainder she kept in her purse for meals and gratuities. The unaccustomed excitement must have suppressed her previous nausea, for she felt remarkably better in a short time.

Dougal was waiting patiently outside, and she smiled gently as he assisted her into the chaise. "Hurry home, Dougal," she said. "We don't want the viscount to learn of my disappearance until later."

She waved to him from the window of the chaise, then with a jerk she was off, out of the inn yard and down the main road. Nell breathed a sigh of relief as she watched the mile markers pass, for every mile away from Lynman was a mile closer to home. The roads were slippery and rough, but she did not concern herself overmuch. Her primary interest was in making as much time as possible before Lynman discovered her absence.

Now Nell had time to ponder her situation. How would Melford feel about having her back? Lynman's taunting words came back to haunt her, and her firm belief that Andrew would come deserted her. Had he believed Lynman's lying note? Perhaps Andrew believed she had chosen to go with the viscount.

Nell remembered everything that had been said in the last days, and soon her mind was in total confusion. Her physical condition was not good and she suffered from depression. The coach rolled ponderously on, and Nell fell into a light, exhausted sleep.

Chapter Fifteen

The morning was well advanced when Melford and Sir Harry whipped through the gates of Lynman's hunting lodge. Neither of the gentlemen were in good spirits since they had been traveling before sunup. After several false leads, they had discovered the direction to the viscount's home and were ready for a mill.

Melford's heart pounded at the thought of seeing Nell again. Snow was piled high on each side of the carriage drive and it was cold and slippery. He brought the carriage to a halt and jumped eagerly to the ground, followed immediately by Sir Harry. There was no one to take the horses, so Melford tied them to the gate and strode onto the wide entrance porch and rang the bell imperiously.

After a short time slow footsteps could be heard coming from the nether regions of the house, and the door was opened by a young maid. Melford said imperiously, "I want to see your master, girl. I am the Earl of Melford."

The girl was obviously frightened and she said, "I am sorry, my lord, but the master is not within."

His face hardened and he said, "I have come a long distance to visit with your master, girl, and I mean to see him."

"But, truly, sir, he is not within." The girl was wringing her hands in her effort to make him understand.

He stared down at her for a moment before asking, "Has he been here? Was he alone?"

She chanced to look into his eyes, and paled at what she saw. Her voice quavered as she said, "Yes, sir. The viscount was here this morning. The lady was with him, my lord."

Melford's face hardened again and he asked, "What happened?"

Before the girl could answer, Mrs. Pemberton came bustling down the hall and said, "You may go, Deidre. I will speak to the gentlemen." She briskly turned to his lordship and asked, "What can I do for you gentlemen?"

Melford said quietly, "I am trying to see Viscount Lynman. Where can I find him? It is imperative that I see him at once."

Mrs. Pemberton stared at him for a moment before saying, "Might you be the Earl of Melford?"

The earl confirmed this with an impatient shake of his head, and the housekeeper went on, "I am sorry to tell you, my lord, that Viscount Lynman is not in residence at present. However," she hesitated thoughtfully for a long moment before saying with resolution, "I am able to state that he has only gone

222

away recently. He was a trifle upset, sir. We have been at sixes and sevens all morning."

Melford stared at her under lowered brows before asking, "Why was he upset? Was there a lady with him?"

Mrs. Pemberton folded her hands across her massive bosom and said, "It was the lady that was the problem, my lord. She left the house before his lordship."

"What the devil?" Melford stared at Harry in confusion.

Harry took up the interrogation. "Ma'am, you said that the lady left the house before the viscount?"

She nodded her head firmly. "My lady had no desire to remain. It was not my place to interfere with her wishes, although I did try . . ."

Harry was becoming impatient. "Well, ma'am, what did you try?"

Mrs. Pemberton looked again at Melford and said, "My lord, when the lady had explained the circumstances to me, I assured her that her husband would be along after her, but she would not wait. She wanted to be away as soon as the roads were open. I could do no more. She hired a chaise in the village and is on her return journey to England."

Mrs. Pemberton looked severe. "Unfortunately, the master asked for my lady this morning, and what with one thing and another, he found out that she had gone. He went after her, and I have never seen a man in more of a fury, sir. If he catches up with her . . ." Her voice trailed off as the situation became clear to them.

Melford thanked the woman for her help and they mounted into the curricle. In the village they stopped at the Red Lion, and Melford went inside while Harry saw to the horses.

From the landlord, Melford heard a strange story. Nell *had* come to the inn that morning, but she had not stayed long. She had taken a bedchamber for a short time before recommencing her journey. The maid told him that she had been ill but refused to break her journey.

Later in the morning Viscount Lynman had appeared and asked questions about her. The landlord had told him about the lady and he had gone (it was presumed) after her. That was all he knew.

The landlord turned away to speak to another customer who had come into the inn, and Melford went back to the curricle, where Harry was waiting patiently.

He took up the reins and said, "Not here. She hired a chaise and is on her way home."

Harry grinned. "That is something at all events."

Melford looked grim and said, "No it is not. Lynman followed her. We must hurry or there will be the devil to pay, Harry." He was silent for a moment before adding, "They said Nell was ill this morning. I wonder what happened?"

Harry shook his head. "Don't be a fool, Andy! You know what females are. Swoon at the drop of a hat."

They were bowling along far too fast on the slippery road when they narrowly missed a coach that was blocking their way. An altercation was in progress and Melford slowed his team, intending to offer assistance.

Although she was apprehensive of her eventual

224

welcome home, Nell was more or less happily ensconced in her chaise. Each milestone caused her to breathe easier. After several weary hours of riding, she stopped for a light meal, then pushed on, meaning to ride through the night if necessary. Now that she had escaped the man, it seemed as if she could not contain her impatience to be home once more.

It was bitterly cold outside, but Nell had a warm brick at her feet and she was not at all uncomfortable. Suddenly a loud report rang out and a voice cried, "Stand and deliver!"

The coach stopped so quickly that Nell was nearly thrown from her perch against the squabs of the chaise. The door was pulled open and Nell gasped in fright. Framed in the lighted opening was the one person in all the world she had no desire to see. The viscount laughed horridly and said, "Thought you would escape me, my fine lady? Well, you are not dealing with a callow youth. I knew you were up to something last night, but I failed to regard it. My mistake."

He motioned to her with his pistol and said, "Out. I now see that I have been too easy with you, ma'am. That can be remedied."

Nell shivered when she saw the steely look in his eyes and she said, "I have no intention of going with you, my lord, so don't think it. This game we have been playing has gone far enough. I mean to go home, with or without your permission."

"Is that so?" he growled. "Out, I say!" He nudged her with the pistol. "I am fast losing my patience with you, ma'am. Now, obey me!"

Nell's eyes flashed as she stared at him contemptuously. "You must think me a great fool, Viscount."

She settled herself more comfortably on the cushions. "You have no intention of harming me." She pushed the barrel of the pistol away from her side.

"Don't try me too far, ma'am. I mean to take you, so come peacefully. I wouldn't like to hurt you, but I will if you put me to it," he told her in exasperation. He grabbed her wrist and pulled her from the coach. "I mean what I say, milady."

Nell was frightened, but she put a brave face on it. She jerked her arm from his grip, nearly falling on her face in the wet snow. Lynman grabbed her again and pulled her to her feet. "Careful, you little fool!" he said. "You will hurt yourself."

Nell raised her chin indignantly and said, "I thought that was the purpose for this exercise, my lord. Or don't you mean to hurt me?" she added bitterly.

"I mean to make you pay dearly, madam, but in my own time. Certainly not here in the cold. Or is that what you want? I could take you now," he told her insinuatingly.

"You wouldn't dare," Nell said, casting a fearful glance at the postboys who were listening avidly to the discussion.

In answer he drew her closer, pressing his head down to hers. Nell gasped and her clenched fist connected with his cheek in a loud crack. She pulled away from his slackened grip and ran back down the road.

In a trice he was after her, dragging her back to his side. She cried out in desperation, "Would you take me knowing I am with Melford's child?"

He halted his movement to stare at her in sudden realization, then with an oath he pushed her to the ground. Turning to his man, who had all the time been holding a rifle on the postboys, he said, "Gather their weapons, Prindle. We are leaving."

At first Nell thought he meant to let her go, but when she saw his eyes, she knew that her moment of reckoning was yet to come. He brought his horse to her side and said, "You will mount in front of me, my lady. I am sorry the accommodations are not better, but I don't feel I can trust those coachmen of yours."

Before she could move, Melford rounded the bend in his curricle and barely avoided hitting them. He beheld Nell in Lynman's rough grasp and something burst in his head. Moving like a cannonball, he crossed the short distance in seconds. Harry tackled the groom, and after a short scuffle, disarmed him, while the entire company watched the scene that was taking place between the earl and Lynman.

Melford pulled Nell out of Lynman's arms and put her behind him. She rushed to get out of the way. His right caught Lynman on the chin and he bored in with a left that put him on the ground. Standing over the recumbent viscount he said harshly, "Arm yourself, Lynman. I have been waiting for this moment for a long time." Andrew took his sword from its sheath and waited while Lynman rose from the ground and took his own sword in hand.

Nell watched breathlessly as they flashed a brief salute and the duel began. Many times the viscount's blade came dangerously near Melford's heart and she closed her eyes in agony. It could be seen after only a few moments that the two men were well matched and that the contest could turn in favor of either.

The clashing of metal on metal was the only sound to be heard in this eerie snow-covered world as the company awaited the outcome of this battle of wills. Melford had his anger driving him on, although he knew he was tiring.

Suddenly Lynman saw an opening in the earl's guard and thrust forward with all his strength. However, just as quickly, Melford parried his thrust, and in an instant it was all over. His blade pinked Lynman neatly in the shoulder. Melford carefully withdrew his blade before wiping it on his handkerchief.

Lynman whitened from the shock of the wound before falling to the ground. While he was still conscious, he heard Melford say, "Stay out of England, Lynman. Should you return in the immediate future, it will be necessary for me to take steps to ensure that you will not be received in society. I hope I make myself clear?"

The viscount opened his eyes and said painfully, "Quite clear, my dear Melford. I am happy to abide by your conditions. I haven't the faintest desire to meet either of you again." He closed his eyes again, and fainted from the loss of blood.

Having settled with the viscount, Melford turned anxious eyes to Nell, who had watched quietly while the duel took place. She stumbled toward him with tears in her eyes. "Nell . . . Nell," he cried. "Are you all right?"

A dark blackness was moving round her head, but with hands held out she went willingly into Melford's arms, crying out, "You came, Andrew! You came," before falling into a deep swoon.

Melford carried her to the chaise, where he entered with her in his arms and held her on his lap.

A white line circled his firmly compressed lips and he gently wiped her forehead with a handkerchief.

Outside, Harry was all business. He made a bandage for the wound from his handkerchief, then retrieved the guns belonging to the postboys. When this was accomplished, he peered into the coach to discover how the reunion was progressing.

He found Nell weeping against Melford's coat, his arms were fastened tightly around her. Harry cleared his throat nervously and said, "Sorry to intrude, Andrew, but something must be done."

Andrew looked blank and said, "About what?"

Astonished, Harry said, "Well, Lynman, you know. Not all the thing to leave him lying in the road, my boy."

Andrew's attention remained with his wife and he said absently, "Then pick him up," before murmuring a soothing word into Nell's ears.

Harry shook his head over this apparent lack of attention to the proprieties, and turned his attention to the still recumbent viscount. Lynman's man was leaning over his body, and Harry said, "He is bleeding a little. I advise you to take him to an inn. We passed one not too far back on the road." He helped the surly man lift the viscount into the saddle, and watched coldly as they set off in the direction from which they had come.

After a moment he went back to the carriage and peered inside. "Melford, Lynman has gone. Shall we resume our journey?"

Melford had recovered himself somewhat and turned a pair of twinkling eyes to Harry before saying, "Would you mind taking the curricle, old friend?"

"Would it matter if I did happen to mind?"

Melford refused to reply, merely staring at his friend with a wide smile, and Harry realized that he was not fully recovered from his ordeal. With resolution he said, "Shall we pause at the next respectable inn?"

Melford agreed. Nell needed to rest after her frightful experience so he said, "Order the postboys to follow your directions."

Harry closed the door and gave the necessary instructions. Soon the little procession moved out. They were far from a respectable hostelry and were forced to travel several hours before finding a comfortable inn for the night. It was nearly the dinner hour when they arrived.

Inside the coach, Nell was blissfully happy. Melford's strong arms held her tightly and everything that had happened was fading into a gray, dreamlike memory. She gave herself up to the pleasure of his presence and refused to talk, pleading faintness.

As for Melford, he too was beyond rational conversation. He thought hazily that he must find out about her misadventure later, but that was in the distant future.

Melford bespoke a private parlor for their convenience, and it was so comfortable Nell could have imagined her experience no more than a bad dream. Andrew prepared a hot rum punch that warmed her delightfully, and she was obliged to blink several times to rid her eyes of the tears that kept appearing. They were so gay, she was determined not to disgrace herself in light of their joviality.

When dinner was over, Nell was truly feeling the force of her exertions and excused herself from further conversation. Melford accompanied her to the door of her chamber and stepped inside for a moment. His dark eyes rested longingly on her face and he said, "You must tell me all about what happened, love, but not I think until we are home. It will be much easier when you have familiar things about you again."

Nell let her hand rest in his and said, "You are right, of course." She smiled shyly at him. It had been so long since they had been together, she had forgotten how his very presence affected her.

He drew her into his arms and placed a hard kiss on her lips, then murmured, "I will not disturb you tonight, my love. You are not looking well, and I don't mean to impose myself on you until you are fully restored."

Nell looked searchingly into his eyes for a long moment before he released her and went out the door. She was aghast at his words, and fell in shock across her bed. Her tears fell like rain as the viscount's words came back to taunt her.

So, she thought, it was really true. In his good nature, he must love her, but he couldn't bear to make her his true wife again. He must believe that she had been, although possibly unwillingly, the mistress of his worst enemy. Nell covered her face with her hands and the tears flowed copiously. Oh, Lynman, she thought bitterly, you accomplished your mission perfectly.

Eventually, she stifled the flowing tears, undressed slowly, and prepared for bed. In the dimly lit room she stared at her reflection in the glass and could not blame Andrew for his feelings. Her pale face framed by an unruly mass of flaming hair hanging down her

231

back caused her luminescent eyes to seem far too big. She was so thin it was nothing short of miraculous that he had even recognized her.

Nell turned from the glass in distaste and climbed into the big, soft bed to lie awake for hours, tossing and turning with hope that Melford might take it into his head to come back.

When morning came, it was a different person who emerged from the chamber. Nell's bruised heart was encased under layers of distrust and pain and refused to be moved by any consideration.

Andrew immediately felt that something was amiss when she came into the parlor, but could find no cause for her coolness. He and Harry teased her as they had the night before, and she smiled gently and responded with merry replies, but all the time Melford could sense her reserve and knew that something was terribly wrong.

As a result of Nell's increased coolness, Melford responded likewise, and soon their conversation was stiff and contained only the essential elements.

Harry's presence actually made things far easier than it would have been had they been traveling alone. Melford was truly puzzled by the turn of events and could not put a name to the cause of the problem. Nell would not release control of her emotions for a moment, and he could not determine the cause for her rejection of him.

Nell was determined not to break down again. It was far too painful. Better by far to pretend that she had never truly loved and been loved by Melford. The secret of their coming child sustained her, and she meant to give to her son (she told herself it *would* be a son) all the love she must deny his father.

Chapter Sixteen

Nell stared out the window of the hired chaise as they crossed the bridge and came into London. She was happy Melford had not decided to return immediately to the Chase, for she could not bear the thought just yet of returning to the place where she had been so happy for so brief a time. Nell repressed a slight shudder. It was almost more than she could bear. To be near him and not feel free to touch him or return his embraces was more painful than she could have imagined.

She peered at him through long dark lashes as he sat beside her. He was staring out the windows. His face was lined as if he, too, had found the journey painful and tiring. Mentally shrugging, she thought, Ah, well. We will all suffer from this dastardly plot.

Soon they were at the door of the town house, and Andrew turned to Nell with a smile. "At last! Thank God this journey is over. We will remain in town for a while, my dear. When you have recovered, we will proceed into Kent."

"That would be best, my lord," she said formally. "I intend to retire immediately. I do believe I could sleep for a week." She yawned.

A footman opened the door and let down the steps and there was no further opportunity for discussion. Andrew assisted her descent and helped her cross the icy cobblestones into the house. Welby was waiting in the hall and greeted them with a warm smile. "My lord, my lady, so happy to see you again." He deftly removed Nell's cloak and bonnet while a footman performed this office for Melford.

"Dashed cold for traveling, Welby, old man," Melford said with a smile. "Perhaps we might have some claret in the library."

The door knocker sounded and Welby admitted Sir Harry, who had been obliging enough to return Melford's curricle, and Melford said, "Join me in the library, Harry," before walking to the foot of the stairs with Nell. He lifted her fingers to his lips and kissed them firmly. Nell could feel the imprint of his mouth on her knuckles after he had released her. "Good night, Nell. Don't rise early tomorrow," he said.

She smiled gently. "Thank you, my lord. I mean to take advantage of your obliging offer." She walked proudly up the stairs to their suite.

Melford watched her ascent with brooding eyes before going into the library, where he closed the door with a snap. Ignoring Harry, who was comfortably ensconced in an armchair before the fire with a glass of claret in his hand, he poured out a generous measure of brandy for himself and swallowed it in one gulp. A second portion followed immediately. When he emptied the glass, he set it down and turned to his friend, who was watching his actions impassively.

"What the devil did that fiend do to her, Harry? Have you ever seen such a change in a person? She won't let me get close to her," he said through clenched teeth. "I wish I had killed the devil!" He dropped into a chair opposite Harry and leaned his head back tiredly.

"No point in that," Harry pointed out logically, wagging his head. "Have to flee the country. Never straighten things out with you out of the country and Nell in. Try something else."

"Try not to be more of a fool than you can help, Harry," Melford said with a wry grin. "What am I going to do with the chit?"

Harry shrugged. "How should I know? You are married to her. Go up there and tell her to come out of the miff or else." He nodded wisely. "Your wife, you know. Must obey you," he sat up with a grin. "She married you twice, so it must not sit too badly with her."

"Damn you, Harry! A pretty fool I must look telling my wife to come out of a miff when I don't have the slightest inkling as to what has disturbed her. For all I know, she may have good reason for being upset!" His face paled at the implication.

Harry easily read his thoughts. "No need to put yourself into a pelter, Andrew. Don't believe such a thing for a moment. Why, the chit would be in more than a snit! I don't believe she would have been able to face you if it *had* happened," he said bluntly.

Melford stared at him for another long moment

before reaching for the brandy decanter again. "I shall go mad," he said. "I must do something."

"You could always ask her. You do have a perfect right to know," Harry pointed out reasonably.

Melford paced the length of the darkened room. "I could not do that. Besides, it would make no difference to me, other than that I should be obliged to make another journey to Scotland. For then I *would* kill him!" he said savagely.

Upstairs, Nell stripped off her traveling gown and pulled on a soft robe she had left behind when she had gone home to the Chase. Her composure was badly frayed by the long days of traveling, and the emotional experience she had just come through. She sat in front of the glass, aimlessly releasing her hair from the severe style she wore while she had been traveling. The auburn mass tumbled down her back and over her shoulders, making her appear even more vulnerable than ever.

After completing her preparations for bed, Nell threw her wrapper onto a chair and climbed beneath the warm covers. She snuffed the candle and lay with her eyes open in the darkness. Unable to weep, she lay in silence, pondering her situation. Only little more than a month past and she had been blissfully happy. Now it would take a miracle to right her in her husband's eyes.

Eventually Nell drifted off to sleep. She did not sense the late night visit her husband made to her room when the house was completely quiet and he was certain she was sleeping.

He stood over her for a long time with only a lighted taper illuminating the room. This he set down far from the bed for fear of waking his sleeping wife. She lay on her back with her glorious hair spread out on the pillows, looking vulnerable and childlike. He finally turned to make his way to his lonely room to lie awake until the small hours of the morning, when he too fell asleep.

Nell slept fitfully, but at last fell into a deep sleep from which she woke late the next morning. She felt languid when she awoke. She yawned and crawled out of bed to ring for her morning chocolate, then jumped back under the covers, for the fire had died down during the night and the room was cold.

Not long after, the maid entered with her tray. She tied back the bed curtains and said cheerfully, "Good morning, my lady. Not feeling ill, I see."

Nell paused in the act of reaching for her cup and said in stricken tones, "It is not noticeable yet, is it Beth?"

Beth stared at her from wide eyes before placing the tray more comfortably on her lap. "Why, what is troubling you, my lady? Surely you aren't afraid."

Nell shook her head and pushed her unruly locks behind her ears before saying, "No, no, no, Beth! You don't see at all? How did you guess?"

Beth smiled. "Now don't put yourself into a pelter, my lady. Only another woman could tell, and only if she is used to seeing such things."

Nell relaxed, then confided, "I have not told Lord Melford, you see. I would not like for him to hear of it from anyone but myself."

The girl grinned and said, "Never fear me, ma'am. I'll not say a word to another soul." She began laying out Nell's morning garments in a brisk, businesslike manner.

Nell took a sip from her cup. "You are right,

though. I have been terribly ill every morning for a month. I don't properly understand it. However, I feel fine this morning." She tasted the bacon and eggs that were so temptingly before her.

The maid nodded wisely. "That's the way of it, my lady. After a while the sickness goes off. Has the babe moved? No? Well, don't worry. Time enough for that, my lady."

Nell picked at her food. "You make it seem so commonplace, Beth. Is it really quite so commonplace?"

The older woman stared at Nell in astonishment. "Has your mama told you nothing about it, my lady?"

Nell dropped her head. "I have no mama to instruct me, Beth. I expect I shall learn, though," she added heartily.

Beth watched her quietly before saying, "You must summon your physician, milady. You should see him before you retire into the country."

Nell shook her head stubbornly. "I don't mean to inform the earl for some time yet. If I saw the physician, it would be necessary, don't you see? I dare not."

The woman clucked her tongue and shook her head but said no more on the subject. Nell rose and dressed for the day.

As usual in winter, the town was very thin of company for most of the ton were at their various country seats. Melford was out when she came down. At his club, she supposed vaguely as she wandered through the empty rooms, having nothing with which to occupy herself.

She was vaguely dissatisfied with herself today.

Had she been at home, she could have occupied herself with a cozy discussion of the menu, or some small housekeeping item. As she had never spent much time at the London house, she was not on terms with the housekeeper. She wandered into the library, where she found a novel by Mrs. Radcliffe. She stifled a derisive laugh. Perhaps it would raise her spirits.

Nell settled into a comfortable chair near the fire and opened her book. Losing count of time in her absorption she remained in the library all the afternoon. When she finished the tale, the shadows had lengthened in the room and it was time to dress for dinner. She rushed out of the library and up the stairs to her room.

Melford had not returned when Nell came downstairs so she had Welby put back the meal half an hour. She paced nervously in the parlor and finally summoned Welby. "Did Lord Melford mention that he would not be in to dinner, Welby?"

He shook his head. "He did not, my lady. He left no instructions, which, if I may say so, is a highly unusual proceeding. Shall I hold dinner longer, my lady?"

Nell considered the kindly face before her for a long moment, then said, "I don't believe so. I will have my dinner now. Apparently his lordship has been detained."

He bowed himself out the door. "Very well, milady."

Nell dropped into a chair and stared unseeingly before her. It was just as she had feared. Melford was unable to take her back and now was seeking his amusement elsewhere. She clenched her fists in despair. Never in her wildest dreams had she truly believed that things could have come to such a pass. And that she should have to endure such humiliation! After the happiness they had shared, it was nigh impossible, Nell thought frantically. Welby came back into the room. "Dinner is served, milady." He regarded her with concern.

The evening passed with no word from Melford. Nell ate her dinner in lonely splendor and retired early to her room. It was the outside of enough, she thought, pulling a brush angrily though her hair. She was unable to sleep and the long hours passed, marked by the tall clock in the hall, which struck the hours for all in the house to hear.

Melford rose that morning out of sorts and displeased with life in general. He had risen a little before Nell and gone off to his club, hoping to forget his troubles in the companionship of his cronies or with a friendly game of cards. He ordered a drink and joined a group at a table. Somehow the hours passed, with Melford drinking more and more. No one noticed his unusual behaviour. Hard drinking was the vogue, and none of the gentlemen found it at all strange that the earl should drown his sorrows or his pleasures in wine.

As the afternoon wore on, some of the gamesters left the club and new ones entered, but Melford remained in his place until Sir Harry wandered in just before dinner. When Melford saw his friend, he threw in his cards and collected his winnings, which had been substantial. They sat down at a private table. For all Melford's drink, no one who wasn't familiar with him could be certain he was even a bit foxed.

Harry eyed him knowingly and said, "Been drinking deep, Andrew? What's up?"

Melford grinned and said, "Why, nothing at all, Harry. Nothing at all. Why don't you join me?" He pushed a glass toward him with a laugh.

Harry stared at him, puzzled, but obligingly tossed off the drink. "Melford, this is doing you no good at all. What is the purpose?"

Andrew refilled his glass. "Does one need a purpose for enjoying good wine, Harry? Come now, drink up," he insisted.

Harry obligingly tossed off the second drink. "I'm blamed if I know what you are at, Andrew. First I find you in your cups and now you try to put *me* under the table."

Melford laughed. "Now, let's not talk about the whys and the wherefores. Enjoy yourself. Only young once." He tossed off still another drink.

Harry shrugged and mentally reviewed his calendar for the evening. He had nothing planned, and Melford *did* need someone to look after him in the mood he was in. He threw himself into the spirit of the task. Calling for cards, they spent several hours playing piquet.

The evening passed. "Well, old boy," Harry said. "Looksh like you done it." He leaned his elbow on the table and eyed Melford owlishly.

Although Melford had been at it far longer than Harry, his speech was remarkably clear. "Done what, Harry? Don't quite take your meaning, old boy." He looked around the room and noticed only a few patrons remaining. "What time is it? I don't see a clock."

Harry pulled his pocket watch from his waistcoat

and opened it. He stared at it for a moment, then turned it over and stared at it. Finally he said, "Blessed if I can make heads or tails of it, Andy. You try."

Melford accepted the timepiece after Harry managed to unfasten the chain from his waistcoat, which was an interminable operation. He too stared at it for a long moment before saying, "It appears to be time to go home, Harry. I wonder if this plaguey thing can possibly be correct?" He placed the watch against his ear and listened intently.

He tossed it to Harry, who dropped it and had to pick it up from the floor, nearly falling from his chair in the process. "What time ish it?" he asked.

Andrew rose, steadying himself by holding onto the table. "It is three o'clock. More than time enough for a respectable married man like myself to be at home." He started for the door.

Harry stared at him and slapped his thigh with a laugh. "Respectably married. By gad, that's rich!" He got up and followed Melford from the room. Melford had received his hat and coat from the porter by the time Harry staggered his way into the hall, but he waited politely for Harry to fumble his way into his outer garments.

The porter, having considerable experience dealing with inebriated gentlemen, asked respectfully, "May I call a hackney, my lords?"

Melford did not deign to answer, but Harry said, "Call a hackney?" He was highly insulted. "Doesh he think we're drunk or shompthin, Andy?"

Melford patted his shoulder solicitously. "I am sure James meant nothing by it, Harry. Did you James?"

The porter grinned at the obviously foxed gentlemen and said, "No, my lord. I—er, merely wanted to be helpful."

"Then you jusht find shome other way to be helpful." Harry turned up the collar on his greatcoat and went huffily down the steps, where he promptly slipped on the ice and rolled the remainder of the distance to the street. The porter helped him to his feet and Harry walked off, a little the worse for wear.

Although in far worse condition, Andrew was determined to see that his friend arrived home in one piece. He accompanied him to his lodgings, then turned his footsteps toward home. Although he had been foxed earlier, the night air sent the drink straight to his head, and Lord Melford was hardly able to walk when he entered his home, although his powers of speech were uninhibited. He proceeded slowly up the front steps, and after several tries managed to unlock the front door. A wave of dizziness overpowered him and he reached out to steady himself on the nearest object, which happened to be a suit of armor placed inside the doorway.

The resulting clatter roused the entire household, accompanied as it was by a string of oaths. Nell was down the stairs in a moment, fearing some accident. She was still tying the belt on her wrapper of emerald satin with rows and rows of lace. Her hair hung round her head and shoulders like a halo. At the sight of her, Andrew was frozen into immobility where he had fallen.

They were soon joined by Welby, the housekeeper, and all the maids and footmen, who gawked at seeing the master in such an undignified position.

Nell was the first to recover and ordered the

housekeeper and all the underlings back to bed. Then she turned to Welby. "Help me retrieve this armor, then you may retire, also."

He offered his arm to Melford, who refused with a few well chosen words, and rose awkwardly before leaning nonchalantly against the wall while they restored the armor. Then Welby excused himself, leaving the earl and countess alone in the great hall.

When they were finally alone, Nell looked Melford over critically. She had never seen him in his cups before, but she knew the symptoms from having dealt with her papa in similar circumstances. He looked so reckless and handsome standing in his wrinkled coat that showed the strain of being worn all day. The pain that had torn Nell's heart disappeared. She had indulged herself with wild flights of fancy, she admitted in a flash. Andrew had not been with another woman, for he would not have returned in this condition. He had still not spoken a word while she looked him over frankly, so she said, "This is a fine time to be coming home, my lord."

He smiled engagingly. "I agree, madam. You are perfectly right."

Nell caught her breath. Even in this moment she loved him passionately. They stared at each other for a long time, and then suddenly time seemed to slip back (back before the viscount had come to destroy the happiness they had shared). She put her hands on her hips and said, "Well, shall we retire? Or do you mean to stand here until morning?" She tilted her head to the side and smiled with a pout.

He continued to smile at her, but shook his head and said firmly, "Sorry my love. I cannot possibly manage the stairs."

Nell sighed but moved closer to him. "Come along." She pulled his arm around her shoulders. "Lean on me, you silly fool."

It took some time for them to navigate the stairs, but they ascended them without mishap. Andrew swore several times and Nell felt like swearing, too before they finally reached his chamber.

Andrew dropped into a chair beside the bed and closed his eyes for a moment. "Pour me a drop of brandy, Nell," he requested.

Nell stood stubbornly in front of him for a long moment. "You don't need any more to drink, Andrew. What you need is your bed."

He laughed, giving her his most charming smile. "Come now, love. You wouldn't deny your husband one little drink, would you?"

With resignation she found the brandy, filled the glass, and brought it to him. He took it with remarkably steady fingers before touching his lips to the inside of her wrist. "Thank you, my beautiful Nell."

She told herself that he was merely foxed and that she shouldn't listen to him. "You won't think so in the morning, my lord."

"Yes, I will," he said drowsily. "The most beautiful woman in all the world, love. Give you my word." He tossed off the brandy in one quick jerk and dropped the glass to the floor.

Nell shook his shoulder in a panic. "Don't go to sleep, Andrew. I must get you undressed. You must help me."

He opened his eyes and said, "Of course, love. Do anything for you. Anything in the world." His words were becoming slightly slurred.

Nell tugged at his boots, but they would not

245

budge. Finally she turned to him in exasperation and said, "Darling, I cannot remove them. You must do it."

"You called me darling," he murmured.

Nell smiled at him. "Do you mind?"

He grinned again. "No, I like it."

Nell laughed, albeit in exasperation, and said, "Good. Now, darling, you must remove your boots for me."

He obligingly pulled them off for her, not without difficulty, while Nell turned back the covers on his bed. When she finished, she said, "Now, love, if you will stand up I will help you out of this coat. Come along." She pulled him to his feet and removed his cravat simultaneously.

In a few moments she had him out of his coat and shirt. She considered leaving his breeches on, when he unbuttoned them and said, "Help me out of these plaguey breeches, Nell. I won't sleep in them and that's that!"

After much tugging and pulling, he was undressed. Nell said, "I am going to bed. Surely you can get into bed without help?"

He laughed knowingly and said, "I don't mean to."

"What do you mean by that horrid remark?" she asked.

He touched the soft curls that hung round her shoulders. "With a wife as beautiful as you are, I don't mean to sleep alone. Get in this bed." His voice was suddenly irascible and Nell judged it best to obey him.

"All right, I will but please get in bed and I will put out the light," she said acidly.

He obliged and Nell slowly removed her robe, aware of his eyes on her noting her every movement. Then she snuffed out the candle and crawled into bed with her husband.

For a moment all was still. Then Andrew rolled over to her and his arms encircled her in the darkness. He murmured, "Oh, God, Nell. I have missed you." He buried his face in her breast and his arms tightened around her more firmly.

Unable to control her movements, Nell's arms went willingly around his shoulders and held him tightly. She whispered, "I missed you too, darling." They remained in a tight embrace and presently fell into a deep sleep.

A persistent throbbing in his head woke Andrew several hours later. He groaned and turned his head a little, trying to ease the pain, when he realized that his face was not in the pillows. He opened his eyes to find a lovely white breast obstructing his vision. He groaned again and thought, Surely I haven't done anything . . . ? Oh God! Realizing that two soft arms were holding him close, he decided to explore further. He lifted his head and his eyes met his wife's lovely, shimmering green eyes. He hadn't realized he had been holding his breath until he released it in a rush. He said the first thing that came into his head, "Thank God," then in an anguished voice, "Oh, Nell!"

Accurately reading his thoughts, Nell's laugh tinkled loudly in the room until he groaned aloud. "Please, love. Have mercy on my head."

"It serves you right, Andrew." Her hand softly caressed the dark tousled curls. "Whatever made you do it?"

He lifted his head to look down at her, and with a rueful smile said, "You. I wanted to forget."

Immediately Nell froze. All expression in her face disappeared and she said, "I—I see." She tried to free herself from his embrace. "Perhaps I should go back to my own room, Andrew?"

His arms tightened around her. "No. Now that I have you here, I am not about to let you go."

A puzzled look crossed Nell's face. "I don't understand, Andrew. Why do you want me to stay?"

His eyes moved hungrily over her face and he asked, "Why do you think, you little fool?"

Nell turned from his gaze. "I truly haven't the faintest idea, Andrew. Perhaps you had better explain."

His hands came up to turn her face back to his and he said, "I want you to tell me something, Nell. I must know." His voice was anguished. "What happened to you when you were away? For God's sake, Nell, what did that fellow do to you?"

She gave him a small smile. "Nothing. Absolutely nothing."

He accepted her statement without a doubt. "Then why have you turned so cold to me? I must know."

It was Nell's turn to be surprised. "I? Cold to you? Why, how dare you say such a thing to me! I never . . . !"

He sat up in the bed and pulled her upright with him. "I am well aware I am not quite myself this morning, Nell. But one or the other of us has gone mad. You certainly have been cold to me! Be truthful with me."

Nell jumped from the bed with a cry. "I am telling the truth, Andrew. I have been behaving as I as-

248

sumed you wished, since you no longer wanted to share my bed."

He was totally flabbergasted. His mouth fell open and it was a moment before he could speak. At last he managed, "I not want to share your bed? Are you mad?"

She tossed her head and jerked the belt tight on her robe. "Certainly not," she said. "You didn't want me after Lynman carried me off, so I maintained my distance. I haven't forgotten that it was I who forced you to continue our marriage. I could do nothing else."

Although his head was pounding, he got out of bed and into his dressing gown. His eyes pierced hers and he said, "What the devil are you talking about, Nell?" He glared at her. "Who said I don't want you?"

Nell felt confused and pushed her hair back from her eyes before saying, "Well, I . . . " How could she ever begin to explain to him? He had not moved from his stance beside the bed, waiting for an answer to his question. She realized that only honesty would serve them now and said, "Lynman told me that you would never believe that we had no . . . umm, well, well, you know, Andrew. I . . . "

He looked piercingly at her and said, "He said that I would never believe that he had not made love to you. Is that it?" he asked bluntly.

She flushed. "Yes. He said you would never want me again and it wasn't necessary for him to actually seduce me."

He came closer and said, "And you believed him?"

Nell shook her head. "I did *not* believe him, sir!"

Andrew rubbed his aching temples, and asked

wearily, "Then why Nell? You are becoming complicated."

She sniffed and lifted her chin. "You should know that, my lord. That first night at the inn you did not come to my room. You gave me to understand that you wanted no more to do with me. What else could I think? You haven't been near me since and I do have a little pride!"

He stared at her for a shocked moment before taking her shoulders in his hands and shaking her fiercely. "I could beat you, Nell, for causing us both so much misery!"

"Why are you angry with me? You caused this problem!"

"My little foolish love, you looked so tired and confused that I could not force myself upon you that night although I desired nothing more than to remain in your presence," he said forcefully.

Nell's eyes lit up with hope, but she said, "You have not come near me since, Melford. Can you explain that?"

"What can I tell you?" Melford asked painfully. He looked down at Nell, then said, "You were so prickly and reserved that I dared not try to reason with you, love. I could not think what I had done to receive such treatment."

Nell took his face in her hands, loving the feel of him. "I'm sorry, my love. I didn't mean to hurt you."

He held her tightly to him before saying, "It is not your fault, my precious girl. That damned Lynman caused everything!"

For a moment they were silent as their lips met in a passionate reunion. Andrew murmured endearments to her, and Nell responded joyously. After a time, Nell said, "I must know about the viscount, Andrew. You owe me an explanation after this contretemps."

Melford stared at her seriously for a moment before drawing her to a chair near the fireplace and settling her on his lap. "It is not a pretty story, Nell. Lynman and I were never friends, but we were not always enemies. Our disagreement began when we found ourselves in rivalry for the favors of a certain lady. I won the lady, but Lynman informed her husband and the affair nearly ended in a duel that would have meant the end of me. However, my father learned about the situation and packed me off to India."

Nell nodded. "That was when our marriage took place."

"Yes. Father said that I had no expectations and I should look to make my future secure. I was quite distraught over the situation and agreed to all his stipulations. Although I traveled about the world after going to the East, I have never returned to England until this trip. I had never thought about my bride at all, I am sorry to say."

Nell's brow was wrinkled but she said, "I begin to understand more about you, Andrew. Were you happy?"

"Not nearly as happy as I have been with you, love."

Nell blushed happily. "Flatterer!"

He grinned at her but returned to his story. "Once Harry and I happened to meet in Venice. Unfortunately, Viscount Lynman was there, too. He was trying to seduce a young lady of good birth, and it was necessary for me to intervene. We duelled on

251

that occasion, also. I won. It is not important to the story to discuss the details, but we met on another unfortunate occasion in India. We seem to have a confrontation each time we meet, but you can see why Lynman hates me so. I confess the feeling is quite mutual."

"He very nearly destroyed something precious between us, Andrew," Nell said shakily.

"Why do you think I made such a fool of myself last night? I have been half out of my mind with worry." He looked at her more directly. "I did make a fool of myself?"

A feathery, delicious warmth filled Nell's heart. It was rather like drinking champagne. She felt giddy and laughed aloud, regardless of Melford's bad head. "That is according to how one looks at it." She leaned back to look at him carefully. "Unless you feel that rousing the entire household in the middle of the night, not to mention knocking down a suit of armor, is making a fool of yourself, I suppose we could say no."

He drew her closer and said, "Tell me the rest. What happened when we came upstairs?"

Nell raised her brows to look at him superciliously. "*When* we came upstairs? My dear sir, you move too quickly. Believe me, it was first necessary to *get* upstairs, which was no mean task, I assure you. You politely informed me that you could not walk up the stairs without considerable assistance."

He raised a brow, and a smile formed on his lips. "Did I ask politely?"

Nell giggled. "Of course. I have never known you to be impolite, milord. With much swearing and not a few oaths, we arrived in this room."

He grinned. "Minx," he said. They clung together for a long moment. "I fear I have shocked you."

"Hardly. It was enlightening to discover how a gentleman comports himself when in his cups."

His palm connected with her rounded derriere. "I love you, Nell. I have been lost without you. I have never been so miserable."

"Brute. How dare you hit me?" she exclaimed. "How much I love you, Andrew! I missed you so."

"We can put this business behind us. Lynman will not trouble you again. I have one thing to say, then I want you to put the entire happening from your mind. Promise?" When she nodded, he continued, "I believe you entirely that Lynman did not touch you, love. But I must and will say this. Even had he taken you, I would want you back because you are my whole life, Nell. I cannot live without you. But I would have killed him. Never doubt it for a moment. I would have killed him."

She put her hands on his face and pulled his mouth down to meet hers. "Do you think I do not know it, you fool? I told him it would not matter, and I told him you would kill him, too. I have complete faith in my husband," she said before his lips touched hers in a passionate declaration of their love.

His arms were circling her, pressing her soft body against his strong muscles. Suddenly he released her, and they both stared at her stomach. Nell's eyes were round in wonder, but Melford was merely curious.

"What the devil was that?"

Nell's face glowed and her lips trembled. "I have something else to tell you, Andrew. I should have mentioned it before, but somehow it did not seem to be the right time." She paused.

With a question in his eyes he said, "Well?"

She smiled widely. "We are going to have a baby."

He was astounded. "What!"

Nell nodded her head firmly. "We are having a baby. That was the first time I have felt it move."

"I can't seem to take it in, love. How . . . ?"

She laughed and laughed. "So, my lord. You do not know where babies come from? Dear me. You *have* lived a monastic existence."

He shook her and said, "Nell, you little minx!" He tried to catch her as she jumped up and pirouetted around the room. "Stop it, you wretch. You might fall. I don't mean for you to hurt my son!" He chased her across the room toward the bed.

Nell laughed over her shoulder. "I am so happy at this moment I could die, Andrew. And I have no intention of harming *my* son!" Feeling dizzy after her pirouetting, she dropped onto the bed.

Andrew leaned over her and said, "Seriously, Nell, you must take care. I mean to have every care of you, my love."

Unfortunately Nell could not compose herself. She asked, "Shall I teach you about love, my darling? I am certain you would enjoy it . . . " She broke off as his lips descended to hers, interrupting her light-hearted raillery. There was no more talking in the room for a very long time. His lordship proved to be a very apt pupil indeed.

Love—the way you want it!

Candlelight Romances

Candlelight Ecstasy Romances